RHAPSODY IN RED

Rhapsody in Red

GEORGE G. GILMAN

NEW ENGLISH LIBRARY
TIMES MIRROR

for:
P.W.
As scared as I was on the
night of the silver gun

A New English Library Original Publication 1976
© by George G. Gilman, 1976

*

FIRST NEL PAPERBACK EDITION JANUARY 1977

*

NEL Books are published by
New English Library Limited from Barnard's Inn, Holborn, London EC1N 2JR
Made and printed in Great Britain by Hunt Barnard Printing Ltd., Aylesbury, Bucks

45002938 7

AUTHOR'S NOTE

On 6 December 1969 there was a rock concert at a California dragstrip called Altamont. As far as I am aware there was no festival of music – or even a town called High Mountain – in the neighbouring state of Nevada at any time during the 1870s.

Chapter One

THE mountain lion was old and ready to die. He had not eaten for more than seven days and the water-hole beside which he lay had been dry for half that time. Not that food or drink could save him now. And old age was not directly responsible for the death that would soon come to him.

High above him, a flight of six buzzards circled – patient, slow-moving dark dots against a brilliant blue sky otherwise blemished only by the angry yellow eye of the cruel sun.

The big cat could not even see the sun, for the morning had not yet run its full course and he was in the shade of a low mesa. But on such a blisteringly hot day as this even the deepest shade offered little comfort. So the mountain lion panted and this constant rise and fall of his exposed flank sapped at the final reserves of energy. It had been several hours since he last had the strength to flick his tail at the swarm of flies that buzzed over his sparse, dehydrated form. And it had been during the night that he had managed, for a final time, to turn his head and raise his body to lick at the wound which would shortly kill him.

It was in his right hindquarter and, perhaps, had he been just a year younger he might have evaded the bullet that caused the wound. Then again, if he were a year older, slower reflexes might possibly have caused the rifleman to make a clean shot. In either case, the big cat would have been spared the agony of a lingering death.

There had been four men, riding north through the lower slopes of the Sangre de Cristo Mountains. Below the snowline and above the great sand dunes trapped at the eastern end of Colorado's San Luis Valley. The cougar had been feeding on a freshly killed mule deer, upwind of the human intruders. An excited shout had warned him and he reacted instinctively – but with the sluggishness of great age. The single shot, exploded in the failing light of early evening by a man bored from a long day of monotonous travel, missed the head and tore deep into the sinewy flesh of the animal's hindquarters.

Fear had powered the escape from following gunfire. Then pain had slowed the bounding run. At first, the big cat had climbed to higher ground, covering terrain he knew. Then the pain diminished but the period of relative comfort was a cruel trick on the animal. The lead buried deep inside him erupted a fatal festering in the surrounding flesh. The infection squeezed evil-smelling pus to the wound opening. And when it was licked away there was always more to replace it. Then other poison entered the animal's bloodstream, to be carried relentlessly to every part of its body: and to the brain.

Thus, as the big cat's physical energy was drained by travel and lack of food, so its mental life was undermined. He came down out of the mountains and dragged himself across the unfamiliar desert. And if there was an animal logic which drove him to do this it had to be that his former domain was now associated with the men responsible for his impending death. Or perhaps it was just that he had lost his bearings. For the pain had returned and it was not just confined to the area of the wound. The poison coursing through his veins engulfed his entire body with searing agony. And so he moved in a desperate effort to escape something he carried with him.

He had stopped at the water-hole in the morning shade of the mesa. But the alkali water was as brutally deceptive as the initial numbing of pain had been. For it served only to prolong the animal's doomed life.

It was possible the cougar knew this but such an animal does not resign itself to anything – until the inevitable becomes the reality.

The buzzards certainly knew it. For they had appeared two

days ago. Always either circling against the limitless blue of the daytime sky: or perched in the night upon the mesa's edge.

The sun reached its noon peak and lanced down to erase the final sliver of shade from beneath the mesa's western face. The big cat blinked, then became rigid, mouth open and arid tongue draped into the gritty sand. The scavengers ceased to circle on the high thermals and seemed to hover: poised for a graceful descent towards the long-awaited meal.

Then the panting began again.

Whatever was moving out there between the fringe of the sand dunes and the first rocky slopes was too far off to be an immediate danger. But the cougar continued to watch, panting harder now that the rays of the sun seared directly on to the length of his body.

High above, the birds resumed their slow circling, taking advantage of the ever-moving air currents. Below them, the blanket of heat pressing against the scorched terrain did not stir. And the shimmer of the slick-looking haze that veiled the far horizons was just an illusion.

So it was the pain-wracked eyes of the cougar, rather than his impaired sense of smell, that told him what was moving inexorably towards him. And he growled just once, his eyes glinting with the dark fires of a depthless hatred. Then, having expressed his feelings for man, the animal died.

The birds swooped.

With intense beauty and grace, they arrowed out of crystal clear space. And, at the moment of alighting on the earth, became cumbersome and ugly. Shrieking with greed, eyes afire and wings flapping, they fought each other for the greater prizes offered by the carcase.

Amid a constant cloud of stinging dust, beaks stabbed and talons ripped at the animal's eyes, tongue and genitals. Hot blood spurted from warm flesh. Strips of meat were ripped from the sides, back, belly and throat – to be gorged by the rapacious birds. Gory entrails were dragged from the massive wounds. The heart, lungs, stomach and liver were torn out of the body, trailing slimy sinews caught in the ravenous beaks. The mutilated carcase was dragged and rolled under the vicious assault of the powerful birds. Drying blood smears were left in the wake of the erratic course, and flies settled on the stains.

Then, less than three minutes after the scavenging had

started, its pace slackened. Their feathers, beaks and talons crusted with crimson changing to black, the birds were near to satiation. But they continued to feed: almost delicately now, as they picked the blood-moist meat off the white bones. And, as they fed, their distrustful eyes cast constant glances southwards. In the direction of the man they had seen long before the dying cougar had become aware of the human intruder's approach.

The man watched the birds from a distance of something over a mile, closing on them at the easy pace of the horse he rode. But his eyes were not distrustful. Neither were they contemptuous of the display of greed. Certainly not horrified at a vivid memory which the sight of the scavengers feeding erupted from the back of his mind. His eyes were merely watchful, from behind a surface veneer of total indifference.

They were eyes of the clearest blue, which surveyed the sun-baked wilderness from under deeply hooded lids. The dominant features of a long and lean face, their piercing brightness was emphasised by the dark colouration of his leather-textured skin. Exposure to extremes of weather had contributed a great deal to the skin tone. But heritage had also played a part, from seeds sown by a Mexican father in the womb of a Scandinavian mother. His hair, jet black and growing to a length that brushed his shoulders, was also inherited from his paternal parent. The rest of his features – with the exception of those ice-blue eyes which were drawn entirely from his mother – resulted from a mixing of the blood of two races.

The cheekbones were high, stretching the skin taut from the firm jawline. The mouth was thin and there was a hawkish line to the nose with its slightly flared nostrils. It was a face that could be viewed as handsome or ugly: depending upon how the beholder responded to the latent cruelty that was at once subtly and clearly visible in the composite of the features. It glinted in the permanently narrowed eyes, was hinted at in the slight twist of the mouth, seemed etched into the lines of passing years and bitter suffering that scored the skin, and threatened from the set of the strong jaw.

At this noon hour of a blisteringly hot day, it was a heavily stubble face – with a thicker growth of bristles along the top lip and curving down at each side of the mouth telling of a moustache. A sweat-run face, with particles of red Colorado dust clinging to the salt moisture and caught in the bristles. The face of a man somewhere between thirty and forty who had lived hard and experienced much – little of it good to recall.

He was a tall man, rising to three inches above six feet. And on such a rangy frame his two hundred pounds of solid weight was distributed to give him a deceptively lean look. His clothing was as travel-stained as the wearer. A wide-brimmed, low-crowned black hat. Shirt and pants of blue denim. Black riding boots without spurs, worn under the pants cuffs. A grey kerchief around his neck. At his waist was a scuffed gun-belt with a holster tied down to his right thigh. The butt of a Colt .45 Navy Model jutted from the holster and each loop of the belt was slotted with a shell.

On his workaday saddle of uncertain age were two canteens, a bedroll, a rope coil and a boot which held a 44/40 Winchester repeating rifle. The saddle was snugly fitted to a sway-backed pinto gelding with a coat only slightly flecked with the white lather of sweat.

The man rode easy in the saddle, allowing his mount to make its own walking pace along a little-used trail between the sand ridges of the dunes and the Sangre de Cristo foothills. Easy, but not careless. His hooded eyes, slit against the sun dazzle, moved constantly in their sockets: from the feeding birds, to the trail ahead, then to either side and, from time to time, glancing over each shoulder.

When he turned to scour the country he had already traversed, his sweat-stained shirt hugged more tightly to his muscular back: and contoured a narrow bulge that extended from under the line of his hair to reach a short way down his spine. A bulge caused by a leather pouch with its mouth held beneath the shirt collar by a beaded thong encircling his neck. In the pouch was carried a wooden-handled straight razor.

When he was a half mile distant from where the cougar had died, his presence put the buzzards to flight. But they had eaten their fill, so their squawks were of alarm rather than anger.

With bloated bellies, the birds were even more awkward on the ground but, once in the air, flight gave them beauty again. For the gruesome gore matted in their feathers and caking their beaks and talons was lost against the dazzling brightness of the sun.

They spiralled upwards, then arrowed into level speed high above the dunes.

The small mesa squatted a dozen yards off the trail to the east and as the lone rider drew level with the mutilated carcase of the animal, he could see it without veering to the side. He saw, also, what had killed the animal. For, during the frenetic feeding, the fatal bullet had been wrenched free of flesh and tossed to the dust close by the trail.

What was left on the bones was not yet old enough to stink of decomposition. But the gelding caught the scent of fresh blood and shook with a tremor of fear. The man smelled the nauseating odour of advanced gangrene and spat into the dust.

'Easy feller,' the man called Edge soothed, stroking the neck of the horse with a brown-skinned hand. His narrowed eyes raked the skeleton and untouched paws of the carcase and identified the remains of a mountain lion. Then he drew back his lips to show a bitter smile. 'Alive he could whip us both. But that's one cat can't be brought back.'

Chapter Two

THE gelding responded immediately to the touch of heels against his flanks, chomping at the bit in his eagerness to spurt away from the scene of recent death. But Edge shortened the reins and tightened his grip: keeping firm control over the spooked horse until the mesa was several hundred yards back down the trail.

A half mile beyond this, the trail swung up from the arid valley floor to make its first assault on the high ground. Far ahead, seeming to be disembodied from the earth and floating without movement on the broiling heat shimmer, sawtooth mountain peaks glinted in the sunlight: their snow-covered slopes holding out a promise of coolness to a man travelling through the furnace heat of the dune country. But the snow-line was still many miles away and several thousand feet above the foothills. And the promise of coolness would certainly turn out to be the reality of bitter cold: harder to endure than the searing heat below.

The tall half-breed was aware of this as he made camp at the side of the trail, in the sparse shade of an aspen grove. And, had he been the kind of man given to flights of fancy, he might have linked the false promise of the snow-capped mountains with the incident of the cougar and drawn a parallel with his life – past, present and future. But, on the few occasions when he did contemplate what had been, was and what might be, his line of thought was always as bleakly realistic as his actual existence.

Wind-snapped foliage from old storms provided kindling for a fire and there was a patch of dusty grass for the gelding to feed on. There was no water, except from the canteens, and he used this frugally – to boil a mug of coffee for himself and to moisten the gelding's mouth. For the snow-capped peaks were too far off to guarantee streams and springs close at hand.

He rested himself and his mount for two hours, until the sun was casting mid-afternoon shadows and was far enough advanced on its slide down the western sky to lose some of its fierceness. But he did not sleep. Instead, as the fire burned low and went out and he finished a meal of jerked beef, sourdough bread and coffee, he maintained his unhurried survey of the country on all sides. And saw nothing that moved until he began to saddle the gelding.

Then, far to the south, he glimpsed an intrusion upon the massive stillness of stoic rock and drifted sand: a tiny black dot drawing nearer and growing larger in perspective as it progressed sluggishly along the trail between mountain and desert.

His deeply lined face retained its impassive set as he cracked his eyes to glinting slits and peered with concentrated effort into the south. The dot enlarged, moving clear of the blurring effect of the heat haze. And a line of lazily rising dust showed behind it: too much dust to be stirred up by a single horse.

He was in a good spot to watch the approach. Some four hundred feet above the valley floor on a flat area of shelving under the humped crest of a rise. Higher than the mesa where the cougar had died and able to see across the tops of the dunes flanking one side of the trail. So he was able to spot the stage for what it was while it was still more than three miles away.

His response was a short-lived grin, expressing mild pleasure, but which did not warm the ice-like quality of his slitted eyes. Then he took out the makings from a shirt pocket and rolled and lit a slim cigarette. He had smoked it, dropped it into the dust and lost the taste of the tobacco by the time the stage halted at the side of the mesa.

Over the reduced distance, he recognised the lines of a heavy,

14

brown-painted Concord coach hauled by a four-horse team. A driver and guard were hunched on the high seat and a male passenger had been squatting on the roof baggage before the stage rolled to a halt. Then the man leapt down and ran to take a closer look at the remains of the big cat. A youngster from the agile way he moved: and something of a dude judging by the glinting trimmings which decorated his clothes.

Despite the silence clamped over the scorching terrain the half-breed could not hear what the youngster was shouting back at the people aboard the Concord. But it was obvious he was making an excited report and that, while the driver and guard were unimpressed, he held the avid interest of the other passengers. For the coach was leaning noticeably to one side as the curious occupants responded to what was being said.

The interest soon waned. The elegantly dressed youngster climbed back aboard as effortlessly as he had left, and the reins were slapped to start the team moving again. Edge lost sight of the coach as it took the curve and started up the grade. But it had drawn close enough by then for him to pick out more detail.

The roof passenger was very young, maybe not yet out of his teens. His hat was a white ten gallon, his shirt and pants were cream trimmed with black and his high boots reversed this. He wore a black gunbelt with a holster tied down to each thigh.

He was perched on some expensive-looking luggage atop the stage, which bore the line's name painted on the doors, and had strips of white canvas hanging along the roof rails.

Contrasting with the youth and outlandish dress of the roof passenger, the driver and guard were both well advanced into middle age and were garbed workaday-style in dark-toned denim.

And, while the kid beamed with pleasure, the older men were sour-faced. The driver appeared to be cursing at the team and the guard was glowering under the strain of maintaining a constant watch on all sides. But he failed to spot the mounted half-breed – merged against the shade of the timber – until the coach lumbered up on to the shelving.

'Oh, Christ!'

His voice was shrill with fear. His red-rimmed eyes ceased their frantic movement and became fixed on Edge. But only his stare was frozen. Without rising, he whirled into a half turn, snatching the Winchester from across his thighs. The rifle was ready pumped and as the stock plate hit his shoulder, he clicked back the hammer and drew a bead on the target.

'Freeze!'

The coach was moving at a crawl as it gained the shelf. The driver half rose, undecided whether to crack the reins for a gallop, or haul on them. He elected to halt the team and sat down hard with the suddenness of the stop.

'Cool word for a day hot as this,' Edge said evenly. 'But the direction you're aiming the rifle is making me sweat more than the weather.'

'You keep him covered, Luke!' the driver growled.

'You damn bet, Augie!' Luke assured.

'Landsakes, a road agent!' This from the young dude, his voice hoarse and his eyes bright with excitement.

The impassive set of Edge's features was altered by a slight turn down at the corners of his mouth. Just enough to express a threatening scowl.

'Wrong, kid,' he countered, shifting his narrow-eyed gaze lazily from the dude, to the side of the coach and then across the twitching face of the driver to settle on the guard. 'But lots of people make mistakes. Some bigger than others.'

'Junior, don't get involved!' a woman shrieked from inside the coach.

The kid glowered a reaction to the order. He was about eighteen with clean-cut good looks and soft fuzz where bristles would sprout in a year or so. A green-eyed blond with some puppy fat still clinging to his six-feet-tall, broad-shouldered frame. The guns in his holsters were matched Frontier Colt .45s with silver-plated frames and wooden butt grips. The bullets around his belt gleamed from polishing. He wore spurs with silver rowels. But the sunlight glinted with most fire on the yellow rhinestones that studded his hatband, shirt-front and boot sides.

The other passengers, peering nervously from the coach windows, were a mixture of men and women. All middle-aged to elderly, and expensively dressed in big city style. The sign on the coach door proclaimed: Western Stage Line. While the canvas banner stretched along the roof rail was neatly-lettered with the red painted legend: Houston Music Society.

'What you want, mister?' Augie demanded. He was a short, fat man of about fifty with anxious dark eyes and teeth that were even blacker from chewing tobacco. There was a bad tic in his right cheek.

'First off, for your partner to aim the gun someplace else, feller.'

'My job to protect the stage and all she carries,' the guard argued.

Everyone stared hard at the half-breed and, with the exception of the dude youngster, all betrayed a degree of fear. The kid seemed to be fascinated, his bright eyes raking over horse and rider to drink in every detail before flicking back to make a recheck.

Edge continued to sit easy in the saddle, feet resting in the stirrups and hands holding the reins lightly as they draped the horn. He sighed. 'Give folks the one warning. Squeeze the trigger or aim the rifle away.'

The guard was a few years younger than Augie. Taller and weighing about the same, but with the flesh packed more solidly to his frame. His features were craggy and he betrayed his nervousness only by a rapid pulse at the side of his neck. He spoke as if he had a sore throat. 'You ain't in no position to give orders, mister!'

Edge showed a flinty smile. 'Made my position clear, feller.'

'He didn't pull no gun, Luke,' the driver muttered, licking his black teeth. 'And he ain't got no help around I can see.'

'Why don't we drive on?' a man inside the coach urged anxiously.

'At least when we're moving there is an illusion of a draught,' a woman added.

'So why's this critter waiting for us, dang it?' the youngster demanded of the driver. He spoke with a croaky tone, as if his voice had only recently broken.

'Junior!' he was warned from inside the coach.

'A ride is all, kid,' Edge answered, without shifting his steady gaze away from the face behind the aimed Winchester.

'All filled up!' Augie said quickly.

'Apart from which, sir, this is a privately hired carriage.' The speaker was inside the coach and out of sight behind the passengers leaning from the windows. He spoke with an educated British accent, slightly slurred.

'Roll her, Augie,' Luke growled. 'Maybe he don't mean no harm, but I'll keep him covered.'

The driver scowled his distrust of the situation, but kicked off the brake and flicked the reins. The Concord jolted forward. Luke swayed with the abrupt movement, and his aim wavered.

The half-breed's moves were a lot faster, but coldly controlled. He thudded his heels into the flanks of the horse as his right hand swept from saddle horn to holstered Colt. The gelding started to respond to the command for a forward lunge. Then reacted to the counter-order as the reins were jerked for a halt. The animal reared high.

Edge stood in the stirrups and pressed his body against the horse's neck. Women shrieked and the gelding snorted. The Colt slid from the holster, hammer cocked and with first pressure taken on the trigger as the gun swung up to the target.

'Sonofabitch!' Luke yelled.

And fired.

It was a panicked shot, an instinctive response to the half-breed's sudden move. The guard cursed again as his bullet thudded into a tree-trunk. His right hand started to pump the rifle's action. The ejected shell case spun in the hot air. The gelding was at full stretch, almost erect on his hindlegs. The Colt exploded, like a muffled echo of the Winchester's report.

The bullet smashed into the lower knuckle of Luke's middle finger. Then burrowed through flesh until it flattened itself against the shattered wrist bone. A dark crimson spray of arterial blood burst from the entry wound. Luke screamed and the rifle leapt from his grasp – as if a tight-coiled spring had been released.

'Damn it to hell!' Augie yelled, slamming on the brakes. Then he dropped the reins and thrust his arms high in the air.

The gelding's flailing forelegs started down through the dust raised by his stamping hindhooves. And two guns fired, their reports merged into a single sound.

Edge felt the horse spasm beneath him, then glimpsed the twin streams of blood arcing to the ground ahead of the animal. He kicked free of the stirrups and powered to the side. The hindlegs of the horse buckled. Then the forehooves slammed against the hard earth. Both cannon bones snapped with a dry crack. The horse snorted its pain, and spasmed again. The half-breed released the reins and folded his knees up to his chest. He hit the ground with a shoulder and rolled.

18

The quivering weight of the horse crashed on to its flanks a part of a second later.

Edge turned over twice and kicked his legs into a splay, an arm shooting out to steady himself. The thumb of his gun hand cocked the hammer. He was in a sitting posture amidst a cloud of dust, three feet from where the horse writhed and snorted with the agonies of bullet wounds and broken bones. The Colt was held out at arm's length, in a rock-steady aim at the youngster on the coach roof.

'Please don't hurt Junior!'

Edge was conscious of the ice-cold grip of rage on his entrails, swamping the pain of his fall. He knew he was just a sliver of time away from killing the boy, but the harsh lessons of a long and bitter experience with violence had taught him more than just how to kill in cold blood. He had also learned how to control the few naked emotions left to him.

The woman's plea played no part in quelling the impulse to kill. Edge simply looked at the boy and saw he was no threat – even though he had a silver gun in each hand. For the ornate Colts were held low and loose, smoking muzzles pointed at his own feet. The youngster's green eyes were wide and bulging with shock as he stared at the agony of the horse.

'You better be as rich as you look, kid,' the half-breed rasped, then swung the Colt and fired at the gelding.

The bullet burrowed into the animal's head by way of his right eye. And another spurt of blood hit the thirsty ground, then became a crawling ooze as the horse was stilled by death.

Edge raked his narrow-eyed gaze over the coach. The young dude was still in shock. Augie was gulping, as if he had difficulty in catching his breath. Luke was grimacing as he held his shattered wrist and sucked at the bloody wound. The passengers inside the Concord seemed petrified by horror.

The kid's voice had a strangled quality as he ended the tense silence. 'I never hit anything alive before, doggone.'

'It's a horse that's gone,' Edge replied evenly as he got to his feet. 'And you owe me for another.'

The green eyes of the youngster met the steady gaze of the half-breed and were trapped. He swallowed hard, thrust the revolvers back into the holsters, and nodded frenetically. 'Sure. Sure, mister. I got lots of loot. I'll pay.'

'You . . . you aren't a . . . a hold-up man, are you?' This from the woman who had warned the kid against becoming

19

involved. She was leaning far out of the door window, the bright sunlight showing the bleach of her hair and revealing the cracks in the powder and rouge pancaked to her fleshy face.

'Just hoped for a ride is all, ma'am,' Edge answered, touching the brim of his hat as he holstered the Colt. 'Fully intend to have one now.'

'Thank God!' the woman gasped, and withdrew into the shade as Edge stooped down beside the dead gelding to unfasten the saddle cinch.

'You got a nerve, after what you done to me!' Luke whined.

The half-breed shook his head slowly as he hauled the saddle and bedroll out from under the carcass. 'Figure I got the right. After what the kid did to my horse.'

'Drive on!' the Englishman urged. 'Tell the man this is a privately hired carriage!'

'Damn right it is,' the injured guard agreed with a scowl.

Augie seemed surprised that his arms were still held high. He brought them down fast and gathered the reins.

The kid made a fast, two-handed draw. He had been standing to his full height among the high-priced leather baggage. But he went down into a crouch as part of the same smooth action of drawing the silver guns.

'Reach for the sky, or I'll fill you full of lead!' he barked. And pushed the Colt muzzle against the nape of Augie's neck.

'Junior!' the fat woman shrieked and the Concord rocked as she lunged for the window again.

The driver vented a low and long-suffering groan. But was unafraid of the guns pressed into his fleshy neck. 'Son, Luke's rifle is down there on the trail,' he muttered. 'I ain't armed. So, 'less you or anyone else aboard reckons to object, I sure ain't gonna stop this here feller ridin' along.'

The half-breed heaved his gear up under one arm and advanced on the stalled Concord.

'You got seventy-five bucks for my horse, kid?' he asked.

The anxious-faced woman at the window nodded emphatically. Then delved a well-manicured hand into a capacious bag hanging from her right elbow. She produced a fat roll of bills and hurriedly peeled off three twenties and three fives.

'I'm responsible for Junior while he's out here,' she explained nervously thrusting the money towards Edge.

'Might be cheaper you carried his guns as well as his money,

20

ma'am,' the half-breed drawled, taking the bills and pushing them into a shirt pocket. 'Obliged.'

'Hey, mister, I'm helping you!' the kid complained. 'Don't you treat me like a baby.'

Edge ignored him and picked up the fallen Winchester from beneath a team horse. The rifle stock was flecked with already dried blood. One-handed, he flipped the gun to complete the action of pumping a shell into the breech.

While he kept his guns pressed into the neck of Augie, the young dude became fascinated by Edge's handling of the rifle. The driver continued to be scornful of the threat he was under, for he had taken a medical kit from beneath the seat and was binding Luke's injured hand.

Edge turned the Winchester and pushed it towards its owner, stock uppermost. Luke took the rifle with his good hand, and groaned as Augie fixed a sling into position.

'Was just doin' my job, that's all,' Luke rasped through clenched teeth.

The half-breed nodded curtly. 'Was just hoping for a ride, that's all,' he countered.

Then he spat on the rim of a coach wheel. The moisture sizzled against the sun-heated metal and the passengers at the windows withdrew hurriedly, expressing disgust. He moved to the rear of the Concord and used the hub and rim of another wheel as footholds to climb on to the roof.

With a grunt of satisfaction, the kid took the Colts away from the driver's neck, spun them by the triggerguards, and slid them smoothly back into the holsters.

'Now we can move, I figure,' he said with a note of triumph in his voice.

'I won't give you no argument,' Edge said as he swung his gear onto the roof and then climbed over the banner-draped rail.

Augie completed attending to Luke, cast a contemptuous glance at the boy and then cracked the reins over the backs of the team as he kicked off the brake. The half-breed sat down hard between a suitcase and his saddle. The young dude, familiar with the uneven motion of the stage, rode with the jolt and then folded his lanky frame down on to the baggage.

'Dang it, I'm real sorry about your mount, mister. But I surely did figure you were fixing to rob us.'

Edge wriggled into a more comfortable position. 'What did

21

you figure my horse planned to do?' he asked wryly.

The boy looked ruefully back along the trail to where dust from under the moving stage was settling on the still form of the fallen gelding. Then he shrugged. 'Dang shame, but Aunt Emma gave you what you asked. No hard feelings, uh?'

'Just the ones against my back, kid,' Edge muttered, and started to rearrange the baggage.

He cleared a space so that he could sit with his back against the saddle and bedroll and with bags on either side to hold him steady. Then he gave a low, contented sigh and tipped his hat forward to shade his face from the sun.

'Doggone it, you ain't going to sleep?' the boy groaned.

'Junior, don't say ain't!' his aunt rebuked from below.

'Junior, don't say ain't!' his aunt rebuked from below.

There was no way around the hump of the rise and the trail curved steeply up the gradient, holding down the speed of the heavy Concord.

'I was hoping for a jaw,' the boy hurried on. 'Chew the fat, like. Landsakes, I figure you got lots of tales to tell. This is my first visit out to the West.'

'It shows, kid,' Edge muttered from under his hat.

Apart from his outlandish garb, which was probably a high-priced city tailor's idea of frontier style, the boy's speech betrayed he was a fish in a new pond. For the country expressions he used sounded incongruous amid other words spoken with the cultured tones of an Eastern university education.

The younger gazed around with gleeful wonder, and sighed. 'Yes, siree, my first time out in the Wild West.'

'Could be you won't get to go back East, son,' Augie growled over his shoulder. 'You keep botherin' a feller that don't want to be bothered. Specially a single-minded feller like him.'

The kid ignored the warning. 'What did you call him, mister?'

'You talking to me?' Edge asked wearily.

'Yeah. First dang time I ever put lead in something that was alive.'

'You said that already.'

'What did you call him?'

'Who?'

'Your horse, mister!'

'Junior, don't bother the man!' his aunt called.

'Horse,' Edge said.

'Yeah!' The boy was growing impatient.

Edge sighed. 'Horse is what I called him, kid. After I got through with bastard. Then sonofabitch if he forgot what he learned.'

'Landsakes, and I thought all you Western critters had names for your horses.'

'I told you, kid. Horse, bastard, sonofa –'

'I mean real names, mister!'

The stage reached the crest of the rise and picked up speed across another area of level shelving towards the next step up into the mountains.

'Most folks live and learn,' the half-breed muttered.

'Some of us the friggin' hard way!' Luke yelled above the noise of the suddenly speeding Concord. Then he groaned as the sways and jolts of motion erupted fresh fires along his arm. 'You ain't friggin' doin' my hand no good!' he snarled at Augie.

'It's a long ways to High Mountain,' came the response. 'And I don't reckon there's no doctor between here and there.'

'You heading for High Mountain, stranger?' the boy asked.

'If High Mountain is what's ahead,' Edge answered. 'But I figure I can take care of what ails me without any doctor.'

'Ain't anything wrong with you that I can see,' the kid countered.

Edge raised his hat a little. Just enough so that he could rake his glinting eyes over the folded form of the richly garbed youngster. Then he spat over the flapping canvas sign at the side of the roof, and allowed the hat to cover his face again. 'That's because you ain't sitting where I am,' he growled.

Chapter Three

EDGE had no control over his imagination when he was asleep: and it was while he was sleeping that his mind was most likely to unlock the countless bitter memories of a harsh past. Thus, as the Concord rattled and creaked over the rising terrain through the furnace heat of afternoon, the half-breed slept and dreamed.

There had been buzzards at the family farm when Captain Josiah C. Hedges came home from the war. Years later, more of the same breed of scavengers had been at Fort Waycross when Edge approached. And, although he had not always seen them, it was inevitable that these feeders on the dead had never been far away from the long and erratic trail the half-breed had blazed or followed from the homestead to the army post.

The farm had been in Iowa, at the end of an exhausting journey from Appomattox: a journey during which hopes for the future had begun to mask recollections of the five horror-filled years which had preceded the peace signing.

But there was to be little peace in the future for the man who was not then called Edge. For he returned to a home that was a burned-out ruin, its blackened timbers crumbling amid charred crop fields. And the buzzards were feeding upon two bodies – one of them the remains of Jamie Hedges. A boy no older than the rich dude who now rode with Edge atop the swaying Concord.

Despite the ravages caused by the rapacious birds, the other body was also recognisable as that of one of the men who had served under the Captain during the War Between the States. One of a group of six troopers who had been inseparable throughout the long struggle between North and South. But, in the first spring of peace, death had set apart Bob Rhett from the others.

Both Jamie and the ex-trooper had been killed by Frank Forrest. Or Billy Seward. Or Scott, or Douglas or Bell. But the name of the man who had fired the fatal bullet into his kid brother did not concern the half-breed. Six men had ridden up to the farm and five had moved out.

All five had to pay for the brutal murder, and the lessons of war had taught Josiah Hedges how to extract payment in the only way that would satisfy him. And they had paid, at the end of another long journey during which the half-breed became known as Edge. They died in a holocaustic torrent of blood-drenched violence that was to set the pattern for his future life. Because afterwards there could be no going back to what might have been. For the vengeance hunt had borne too close a resemblance to events of the war. And, although he killed for a cause much stronger than that which had excused such violence before Appomattox, the law accepted no justification for his actions.

And Edge was branded a murderer.

Not, by a quirk of cruel fate, for slaughtering those who had ended his brother's life. Instead, he was wanted for killing a man who got in his way as he searched for revenge. And, since then, many other men had become buzzard meat because they had blocked the half-breed's path.

Once, he had made an attempt to recapture a semblance of what might have been: and had almost paid for the murder he had forgotten. But he had been sick then. Riding from a town called Rainbow with a bullet wound in his body, stinking of the same odour of gangrene that had clung to the carcase of the mountain lion. And, his mind burning with the effects of the poison, it had been instinct rather than a clearly formed plan which had turned him away from violence towards a remembered promise of home and peace.

But fate, in the guise of favouring him, had twisted to snatch

25

him away from the posse sent to capture him: only to plunge him back into a constant blood-bath of new death and destruction.

And he had accepted it and dealt with it, surviving each time to face a future that offered nothing good. Until his aimless trail took him to the Dakotas, where he married Beth Day. But those few short weeks of peace and happiness in the Badlands proved as much a false promise as his journey away from war had been. Beth died, more cruelly than Jamie had done. And, because the finer human emotions aroused in him by his wife forced him to bear the responsibility for the way she died, her death had dehumanised him more than any other single event in his harsh life.

He left the Dakotas, with violence dogging his tracks and lying in wait for him: resigned to existing as the complete loner – bitterly aware that anything he should choose to love, or even desire, was destined to be put into his grasp then brutally snatched away. Thus, he was a loser as well as a loner, insulting himself against the world with an almost impenetrable barrier of bitter cynicisms and backing this with brutal action when necessary.

A trained killer who honed his animalistic skills almost as frequently as he sharpened the blade of the razor carried in the neck pouch. Never gaining anything except survival to face the challenges of future violence.

Just once more, as he drifted from state to territory, zigzagging from the Middle West to the Pacific Coast and from Mexico to Oregon, a link with the past had appeared outside of the bitter dreams. A man had come looking for him – to arrest him for that ancient murder and to gain revenge for what had happened to Beth Day. The man died and another quirk of turn-tail fate had made his death an accident.

But that was long in the past now. Like so many other deaths – none of which had been accidents – which marked the aimless trail ridden by the tall half-breed since he buried his brother on the Iowa farmstead. Because of the kind of man he had become, he remembered only Jamie, the troopers, Beth and his challenger for her love. Those who, by their living and their dying, had forged his cruel destiny. The others who had spilled their life's blood across the wastelands of time between, were faceless ghosts, lacking substance even when sleep unlocked his memory.

They were there, of course. The people, the places they had died, and the manner and reasons they had died. For everything a man experiences is stored in his subconscious. But in the mind of a man like Edge, the death of another human being registered no more vividly than the passing of a wounded mountain lion. Unless he had loved or felt some degree of respect for the victim.

He could remember Sullivan and the fat man's bunch of killers, who had also seen the buzzards at Waycross: and who had all died on the gruelling trek across Arizona towards Fort Hope. But their blood was still fresh on the ground.

'You don't look like somebody interested in music, partner.'

Edge had slept as much as he needed. And no danger had threatened while sleep eased the weariness of a long ride out of his mind and body. For when he slept – dreamless or otherwise – he remained just below the level of consciousness: and could be triggered awake to instant awareness and total recall by the first hint of a threat. The result of a lesson of war that had proved as invaluable as his killing skills during the blood-run aftermath.

But he awoke to relaxation now, easing his eyes open to the darkness of the inside of his hat. And knew at once that he was sharing the uncomfortable roof of a stage with a talkative and impulsive rich kid from an Eastern city.

It was as he stretched sleep-stiffened limbs that the young dude addressed the half-breed.

'You ain't going to sing to me, are you, kid?' Edge growled as he pushed his hat back on to his skull.

Instinctively he checked that the Winchester was close at hand and that the Colt was still in his holster. He could feel the slight pressure of the pouched razor against his back. Then he raked his narrowed eyes over the terrain on all sides.

'Landsakes, no! Just wondered why you were heading for High Mountain, partner.'

The Concord was still rolling along an old trail, a lot higher up in the Sangre de Cristo Mountains now. It was late afternoon and the sun was hidden behind a line of ragged ridges to the west. The rocky ground curled up higher still in the east to form a deep valley. The trail, which showed few signs of recent use, ran arrow straight through the centre of the valley floor, rising gently to go from sight over a crest. Beyond the top of the long rise, the snow-capped peaks of the highest mountains seemed as far off as they had from the fringe of the dune country.

The lack of sun and the high altitude put a fresh chill in the air that dried sweat and raised goose bumps. And there was no longer any heat shimmer, so that unshaded features of the barren landscape stood out in stark clarity.

'Son!' Augie snarled without turning around. 'Didn't them dime novels teach you not to ask questions of a man?'

Luke did glance over his shoulder: and grimaced as his injured hand complained at the sudden movement. He was pallid beneath the bristles and trail dust and the pain had dulled his eyes. But emnity towards the half-breed showed a flicker of fire for a moment.

'He already made it plain he ain't a talker,' the guard rasped before turning gingerly to face front again.

'You were tired then,' the boy said hurriedly, his eyes still bright with excitement as he gazed with fascinated interest at Edge. 'I ain't holding it against you, what you said. But if a man don't feel like talking, that's all right with me, mister.'

The half-breed finished making his survey of the surrounding country and started to roll a cigarette. 'Like that better, kid.' He lit the smoke.

'What?'

'Mister. Or Edge if you want. Partner of mine you're not.'

The kid was not offended. He nodded vigorously and wreathed his unblemished face with a broad grin. 'Sure. Edge.' He paused. 'That sounds fine. Yeah, I reckon I'll call you Edge. You're the first feller I seen that's got them.'

Edge was in process of ejecting the spent shell from his revolver and pushing a fresh round into the chamber. 'This is the West, kid,' he reminded wryly. 'Where men are men and the sheep are nervous. We all got them.'

The youngster blinked, then shrugged his lack of understanding. 'I mean those eyes of yours, Edge. The kind that's filled with far horizons.'

'Filled with what?' the half-breed muttered.

'He's a big reader,' Augie said sourly, and bit off a chew of tobacco.

'My name's Rydell,' the kid said. 'Hiram Rydell, dang it. But my Pa has the same given name, so I mostly get called Junior by my folks. I don't mind that so much, on account of Hiram ain't got a ring has it?'

'Long as Mrs Hiram Rydell's got one,' Edge answered with a hint of a smile.

Augie spat some juice. 'One word of encouragement and he goes on for hours.'

'Don't bother the man, Junior!' Hiram's aunt cautioned. 'And don't say ain't.'

Hiram ignored both interruptions. 'Was born and raised in New York City. Over on the plush West Side. But I've wanted to come out here to the frontier lands for as long as I can recall.'

'Seems you're the only one happy you made it, kid.'

The youngster's mood was deflated a little and he scowled. 'That sure is right. Edge. Tenderfoot like me, I – '

'Tender what, Hiram?'

'Tenderfoot, Edge. A tinhorn.' He looked puzzled.

'He's puttin' you on, son,' Augie growled, and spat more tobacco juice. 'He knows what you mean.'

The kid shrugged, then grinned sheepishly. 'Yeah, all right. I guess I have to get used to being ribbed all the time, dang it. That or being bawled out. On account of I ask questions. But how's a feller to learn things if he doesn't ask questions?'

'Doing things is the best way I know,' the half-breed told him.

Hiram sighed. 'I try all the time. But I keep doing the wrong things, dang it. They work out mighty fine in the dime magazine stories. Out here in the real West, though . . . Landsakes, it ain't nothing like it's made out to be in the books.' Abruptly, his handsome young face brightened with a beaming smile. 'Leastaways, it wasn't until I ran into you. Edge.'

Luke turned his wan face towards the roof passengers again. 'Kid, he sure don't seem like no Western novel hero to me,' he rasped.

'You ain't read a book in years, Luke,' Augie accused, with another spit of juice.

Edge arced the cigarette over the side of the coach. 'Maybe I'm a new kind,' he suggested evenly, curling back his lips to show a cold grin.

'That stuff about not calling you partner, Edge,' Rydell hurried on. 'That's the kind of thing I have to learn. Landsakes, everyone that's on the same side calls everyone else partner in the dime novels.'

29

'Figure most of them say "landsakes" and "dang it" all the time, too, uh?'

The kid showed another sheepish grin and for a long time there was just the creak and rattle of the big Concord to disturb the high country silence.

Far ahead, the snowy peaks became veiled in the broiling mist of a storm, and the darkening blue of the sky retreated before the advance of a spreading cloud bank.

'You just drifting up to High Mountain, uh?'

Edge, Augie and Luke had donned sheepskin coats as the wind scudding the clouds dropped lower and cut along the valley. Hiram had merely tightened the cords holding the big hat on his head.

'No, Hiram. Riding a stage.'

The half-breed continued to scour the ridges and rock outcrops. He had trusted his instincts for imminent trouble while he slept, backed by the knowledge that Augie and Luke were keeping watch over country they distrusted. The driver and guard were still as alert as ever, but Edge never relied on others unless he had to. Apart from which, vigilance was an unbreakable habit.

'Looking for work?'

'First for a horse, kid.'

'Come far?'

Edge fixed him with an icy gaze that caused Hiram to swallow hard. 'You won't learn nothing worthwhile from my past.'

He had come a long way; from the isolated Fort Hope in Arizona to this bleak range of mountains in Colorado. And the ride had been trouble free until he was mistaken for a hold-up man. There had not been any trouble at the army post either, while he worked for two weeks busting mustangs into cavalry mounts. It had not been the kind of work he liked doing, but it was the only kind available and he needed the pay to buy a horse, gear and supplies – to replace what he had lost because Sullivan had wanted to kill a woman.

Some renegade Apaches killed her before Sullivan had the chance, but Edge considered he had lost more, and not just a horse, gear and supplies. A ten-thousand-dollar bankroll which he had planned to use for yet another attempt to put down peaceful roots. But the banshee laughter of the cruel fate which ruled his destiny had once more been drowned by the crashing of gunfire and the screams of the dying. And the

30

bitterness of defeat in all things save survival had hardened the half-breed still more.

'Okay, Edge,' Hiram allowed. 'I won't ask you no questions about that. But I reckon you'll get work at High Mountain. What with the Music Festival happening there.'

Edge recalled the canvas signs hung from each side of the Concord, and what the kid had said as he saw the half-breed was awake. 'Poker's the only thing I play, Hiram.'

'Aw shoot, you're putting me on again,' the youngster groaned.

'I hear they ain't relyin' on the local sheriff, Edge,' Augie offered as the team hauled the Concord close to the top of the long rise. 'And you got what it takes to make a guard, I reckon.'

'Quit it, Augie!' Luke snarled. 'We don't owe him no favours.'

The half-breed felt a vague stirring of interest, but not sufficient to pursue the matter.

'Unfriendly critter, ain't he?' Hiram muttered, probably quoting an entire line from his favourite reading matter. Then he grinned. 'But I guess you don't give a damn about him?'

'Junior!' his aunt shrieked as the coach crested the rise, to enter a low-sided gorge at the foot of the downgrade beyond. 'That is a cuss word!'

'Under a bad influence, I feel,' the Englishman added, his voice more slurred than ever.

The Concord tilted to one side as the heavily built woman thrust her head and shoulders out of the window and craned her neck to stare up at the roof.

The kid grimaced, but flinched away from the powerful glare of his accuser. 'Aw, shoot!' he muttered.

'Ain't all crap you talk,' Edge rasped. And reached for his booted Winchester.

Two other rifles spat death, and the Concord was suddenly filled with screams of terror.

Aunt Emma's bleach blonde hair was abruptly splashed with dark crimson. Her mouth was still open to express shock at Hiram's bad language – and the bullet that had shattered her skull broke her dentures as it crashed through the roof of her mouth, then was ejected amid a spray of blood and fragments of enamel as a dying breath was expelled from her lungs.

The second shot ended Luke's life as Edge pumped the action of the Winchester. He was hit in the chest, the impact of the bullet flinging him backwards across the roof of the coach.

'She's dead!' Hiram shrieked, and half-rose to go for his fast draw.

Luke's body slammed into him and the kid was pitched hard to the boot of the coach.

'Surrender!' the Englishman yelled.

The boulder slammed to the trail just ten feet in front of the lead pair of the team and the horses reared in terror.

'Bastards!' Augie snarled, the wad of soggy tobacco rocketing from his mouth.

The searching eyes of Edge had spotted the man using a rifle to lever the boulder off the cliff. And he blasted a bullet into the heart of the masked man as the Concord came to an abrupt halt.

Luke's body was hurled forward, to crash down on to the drawpole between the back pair of horses. It hung there for a moment, then slammed to the ground. Both animals reared, and the guard's unfeeling head was burst open by a flailing hoof.

The half-breed powered to the side, knocking aside baggage as he rolled over the rail and dropped to the ground.

A fusillade of shots exploded as he tumbled, bouncing off the dead woman slumped out of the window.

'Jesus!'

'You friggers!'

'It's gone wrong!'

Icy needles of sleet joined the assault of the wind rushing down the gorge.

'Bastards, bastards, bastards!'

Edge hit the rocky ground in a crouch and powered into a head-over-heels roll. As his vision was blurred by the speed of motion, he recognised Hiram's voice yelling above the crash of gunfire and the screams of the passengers. He came to a bone-crunching halt against the base of the rock wall and swung the Winchester – to explode a shot towards the stab of a muzzle flash.

A bullet blasted rock splinters an inch to the left of his head. But, as his glinting eyes found focus again, he saw his shot penetrate the face of a masked man. The man hurled away his

32

rifle, threw his hands to his face, and corkscrewed to the ground with a shrill scream.

Edge swung his head and rifle in another direction: in time to see Hiram Rydell kill his first man. The ambusher had been hit already and was sitting on the ground. His rifle was gone and he was using both hands to try to stem the blood oozing from a stomach wound. Hiram was drawing himself up to his full height from where he had fallen at the rear of the Concord. He was silent now, with both silver guns aimed rock steady at the injured man.

The expensive Colts were still smoking at the muzzles. Then, as the doomed man looked up – expressing a silent plea for mercy with his eyes above the kerchief mask – the guns spat bullets. The man's eye sockets became dark pools of crimson. The next instant his brains spewed from the twin exit wounds and he toppled back to cover the gory mess.

'All right, I give up!'

Hiram had taken only a part of a second to complete his kill, and the narrowed eyes of the half-breed were searching for new sources of danger before the dead man measured his length on the ground.

'I'm the last one!'

The sleet was falling thicker and faster, lancing down at an angle before the force of the wind, stinging exposed flesh and pasting clothing to the body. The fourth ambusher stood rigid beside the toppled boulder, his rifle held two-handed high above his head. His eyes were wide with terror as he stared at the muzzle of the half-breed's aimed Winchester.

'Obliged for the information, feller,' Edge told him evenly, and winced as he got to his feet. 'Eases my mind if not my body.'

The survivor was dressed the same as his dead partners, in an ankle-length black coat with the collar turned up to brush the underside of his hat brim. There was a gunbelt slung around his waist on the outside of his coat. He wore gloves, so that the only flesh exposed to the weather was the top half of his face above the mask.

'Damn it, I figured we was all gonnas for sure!' Augie yelled.

He scrambled down from the coach and hurried in a half circle to get behind the captive. Then lunged in close, plucked the revolver from the holster and the rifle from the gloved hands. Then:

3

'It's all okay, folks! We bagged us the whole bunch of 'em!'

Edge canted the rifle to his shoulder, and massaged his bruised right hip which had suffered the brunt of both recent falls.

Hiram's spurs jingled as he turned, spun his guns on the way to the holsters, and moved towards the side of the coach. There was an expression of grim hardness on his features, which somehow looked many years older than before. But there was also a suggestion of the tears of grief behind his green eyes. As he started to ease the body of his aunt from its undignified position across the window frame, the other door of the Concord swung open and the passengers disembarked into the wind-driven sleet.

There were seven of them – five men and two women. All middle aged to elderly and attired in high-priced clothing unsuited to the change in the weather. Tweed suits and cravats for the men and silk gowns for the women. Derby hats and sun-bonnets. The clothes were powdered with dust from the long trip, and the sweat of the day's heat and the evening's terror was a dry sheen on bristled and painted faces. Throats pulsed, eyes darted this way and that and tongues licked trembling lips. Low gasps and a single shriek sounded as fear-filled eyes located the bloody-pulp of Luke's head.

'If I may speak on behalf of my fellow passengers, we owe you gentlemen a debt of gratitude.'

The Englishman was least frightened of the elderly passengers. Close to sixty, he was a tall man with a build that was muscular turned to flabbiness. He had the ruddy complexion of a heavy drinker, but his grey eyes were bright and clear. His sideburns were grey, linking up with an even thicker moustache that was mottled grey and black. He carried a silver-topped cane in one hand and a drinking flask in the other.

'Thought it was you wanted to surrender, feller,' Edge growled, and spat.

The red-faced man seemed on the point of an angry retort. But he brought himself under control with a slug from the flask. 'A man must temper his will to fight if there are ladies who could be further endangered, sir,' he said, very distinctly as he made an effort to keep from slurring.

'You reckon we should hogtie this here bastard?' Augie asked.

'Driver, there has been enough foul language!' the Englishman chided.

'Leave the sidewinding critter to me!'

All attention swept towards Hiram as the kid straightened up from beside the body of his aunt. His eyes were red-rimmed, but if he had cried the sleet that washed the tears from his face: and there was no sound of grief in his harsh tone.

'Get away from behind him!' the youngster ordered Augie.

The wind gusted stronger and the elderly passengers held their hats to their heads.

'A prisoner's got rights!' the stage driver yelled.

Hiram advanced slowly along the side of the Concord, eyes not blinking against the attack of the minor blizzard. 'They killed my kin,' he croaked, and did his two-handed draw.

'Law'll take care of him!' Augie shouted, but leapt to the side.

'Stop him!' the prisoner shrieked, suddenly trembling. He dropped his hands to his face and dragged off the kerchief. 'Please?'

He was about the same age as Hiram. But paler and thinner. There were tears in his dark eyes and as his lips quivered, spittle ran from the corners of his mouth. He thrust out his hands, palms uppermost in a gesture of helplessness.

'Get hung for sure!' Augie yelled.

Hiram showed again his ability to ignore interruptions that didn't suit him. He continued to advance, alongside the quietened team now, his matched guns levelled at the quaking man.

'Edge!' the ruddy-complexioned foreigner roared. 'This must be stopped. The villain must be handed over to the authorities.'

The other passengers were dumbstruck by the menace of a new evil lurking over the carnage that had erupted in the sleet-veiled gorge.

'Got business of my own to attend to,' the half-breed answered evenly, and started to turn away.

'Please!' the ambusher shrieked, and lunged forward.

His aim was to reach whatever protection was offered by the huddle of elderly passengers. All save the Englishman scampered away with choked gasps. The moustached man held his ground, dropped the flask, and yanked at the silver knob of his cane.

35

'Hold it!' Augie yelled.

The handle snapped away from the cane – and a length of steel blade started out of the wood.

But Hiram's guns exploded before the sword was clear of its unorthodox scabbard. Edge halted in his half-turn as the ambusher was hit in the hip, twisted with a scream, and went down. The man's belly took a bullet. Then his chest, left of centre. He was dead as he sprawled to his back. But the young dude's hatred was not quenched until he exploded a final shot into the throat of the corpse.

For a moment, Hiram stood stock still, his red-rimmed eyes empty of expression as they stared at the blood oozing from the dead man. Then excitement and pride were etched into his features as he swept his gaze over the shocked faces of his fellow passengers. But his new mood did not reach fulfilment until his gaze found the impassive half-breed.

'Hell, he sure got what was coming to him, didn't he?'

'Figure that's a matter of opinion, Hiram,' Edge muttered, glancing from the scowl of Augie to the varying degrees of shock expressed by the faces of the passengers.

'Doggone it!' the kid snarled, and spun his guns to the holsters. Then whirled and lunged towards the Concord.

The Englishman shoved the sword back into the stick and retrieved his flask, to suck greedily at the liquor inside. Augie hurled away the confiscated guns and began to drag Luke's body from under the team. The men huddled together and spoke soft words while the two women knelt in silent prayer.

'Look what they did to her!' Hiram demanded at the top of his voice, drawing all attention back to himself. 'They had to pay! Every last one of them.'

The kid was holding the stiffening corpse of his aunt, her bulk and weight seeming to cause him no problem as he held her out in justification for the murder.

'A man's gotta do what a man's gotta do! Ain't that what's said, Edge?'

The half-breed pursed his lips as he turned up his coat collar against the bite of the wind-driven sleet. 'Figure it's written more than it's said, Hiram,' he answered evenly.

'It matters not, young man,' the Englishman announced with a weary sigh as he lowered the now empty flask from his lips. 'What is done is done. All that does matter is that we triumphed over an evil enemy. We were outgunned and facing defeat. But the man most of us have abused gave us the will to win.'

He turned unsteadily, then bowed stiffly towards the seated half-breed. And belched.

'I reckon I put in my two centsworth!' Hiram claimed as he lowered the body of his aunt to the water-run ground.

'You and Aunt Emma both,' Edge allowed with just the hint of a quiet smile in the set of his mouthline. 'Where there's a will there's always relatives.'

Chapter Four

THE wind strengthened and hurled the sleet even harder and heavier into the gorge, the ice-cold downpour creating a fast-flowing stream that rushed around the booted feet of the living and washed the crusted blood off the dead. It also hastened preparations for resuming the journey to High Mountain.

But Edge was not aware of this until he returned to the stalled Concord after back-tracking out of the gorge to go in search of four horses and a dead man. He found the geldings ground-hobbled a hundred feet back from where the corpse was slumped on the rim of the gorge. He led all the animals down to the coach again, with the stiffening body of the hold-up man lashed to a saddle.

'We thought you had deserted us, sir,' the Englishman called as the half-breed hitched the quartet of horses to a rear spring of the Concord.

'Told 'em you hadn't,' Augie supplied.

Both were on top of the coach. The baggage had been re-stacked to clear a space and some of the cases had been opened to provide clothing as makeshift shrouds for the bodies of Luke and the woman. One tightly wrapped form was already lying on the roof. Hiram and a couple of the rich old-timers were in process of raising the second.

'We just want our own dead, Edge,' the kid growled. 'Don't want what's left of these varmints.'

'Ain't what you folks want concerns me,' the half-breed answered as he checked that the horses were securely hitched. Then moved towards the corpse of the second man he had killed. 'Maybe the law wants these fellers – for a price.'

The shrouded corpse was safely delivered into the hands of the men atop the coach and Hiram suddenly expressed another beaming grin. But it was an expression that no longer held the mildest hint of naïve wonder. 'What they call bounty money, uh?'

'Right, kid,' Edge confirmed as he began to lash the body to another saddled horse. 'And if you feel the calling, those two are yours.'

'Dang it, why didn't I think of that!' Hiram exclaimed, and whirled to splash through the rising water.

'Son, your father is a millionaire!' the Englishman roared.

'And it's about time he didn't have to pay my way no more!' the youngster yelled back, stooping to lift the first man he had killed.

Edge climbed up to the seat vacated by Luke as Augie resumed his accustomed position and bit off a chew of tobacco. All the coach passengers were already inside out of the weather as the Englishman lowered himself to the water-run ground.

'You, sir, are owed a debt by us all!' he proclaimed breathlessly, glaring up through the driving sleet. 'But that does not prevent me from thinking that you set an extremely poor example to that young man. He is becoming a younger shadow of you. Why, he's even talking like you!'

'I ain't owed anything by anybody, feller,' Edge replied evenly without looking at the pompous old man. Then, to Augie: 'You want to get this rig rolling? Before it starts to float the wrong way from where we're headed?'

'I been worryin' about that myself, young feller,' the driver muttered.

'Worrying never got anybody anywhere,' the half-breed countered.

'Okay, men!' Rydell yelled as he took his place on the roof and the Englishman climbed into the coach with an angry slam of the door. 'All done. Let's hit the trail. Head 'em up, move 'em out!'

'That's for cattle,' Augie growled, then kicked off the brake and cracked the reins over the backs of the team.

'Beat a rug, this strip of country sure is packed with a mess of trouble, ain't it?'

Augie mouthed an obscenity as the Concord jolted forward, the hooves of the team raising spray to add to the sleet beating into the faces of the men on the seat. He steered the horses carefully through the space between the fallen boulder and the gorge wall, then sighed. 'Don't never rain but it pours, son,' he growled.

Edge remained silent, conscious of a deepening sense of resentment he felt towards the young New York dude. The stuff-shirted Englishman was half right. When Hiram was not quoting phrases from the worst kind of Western pulp novels, he did ape the half-breed's way of talking. But, more important than this – and it had nothing to do with imitation – the kid's actions and reactions during the hold-up attempt had been like a frantic tableau from Edge's own past. And, as Augie skilfully handled the team and Concord against the forceful rush of water, the half-breed was prepared to admit that the foreigner was totally right and possessed the perception to witness the acts of the older man and recognise that once he had been as impetuous and lacking in self-control as the youngster.

Edge hunched lower in the seat and crushed his hat harder on to his head as the Concord lumbered out of the gorge. The wind gusted with unhindered power across a barren mountain slope, as if seeking to wrench the men off the coach: and hurled sleet turned to hail with stinging force against their faces.

'The hell with him!' the half-breed rasped.

'Who?' Augie yelled.

Edge hadn't realised he spoke aloud his uncharitable thought. 'Feller with the moustache right around his head,' he muttered.

'He's from England!' Augie shouted above the howl of the wind. 'One of what they call noblemen over there! Lord or somethin'! Got a double-barrelled handle!'

'Finn-Jenkins!' Hiram supplied from behind the seat. 'Critter called a Baron!'

'What's that you say he's called, son?' Augie yelled.

'Baron!'

'Damn shame his mother wasn't,' Edge rasped, more softly,

40

so that the raging of the weather and noise of the rolling coach masked his comment.

Then he shook his head, irritated at himself. The British nobleman had said nothing of which the half-breed was not already aware. He had merely spoken the truth and by so doing had emphasised in Edge's mind the uncharacteristic ambivalence he felt towards Hiram.

He had gotten to like the kid during the hot and uncomfortable ride through the afternoon for his naïvety and his eagerness to learn. But it was possible to like somebody from a distance, without involvement. Then had come the ambush and, in the process of slaughtering the attackers, the kid had gotten close enough to Edge to pierce the defensive barrier against involvement. They had saved each other's lives and flying lead had forged an affinity.

On the foundation of such an affinity, it was dangerously easy for a relationship to be built: an involvement which, Edge knew from bitter experience, would be doomed to end in tragedy. And he had sworn never to suffer that brand of anguish again – until his cruel ruling fate proved once more that even his firmest intentions were destined to fail.

So the resentment had been born.

The storm ended more suddenly than it had begun. As the Concord crawled sluggishly higher into the mountains, the sleet and hail was driven away to the south. The norther died with a final mournful howl of defeat and the high clouds raced for a minute or so more, then began to swirl slowly and break up across the face of an almost full moon. The air became eerily still, and starkly clear as blue moonlight gained unobscured access to the mountain landscape. Frost crystals started to sparkle more brightly than the folds of snow draped atop the highest peaks.

'Well, I'll be!' the kid gasped, gazing around in wonder at the cold beauty of the bleak scene spread out on all sides.

'You'll be what, Hiram?' Edge growled.

'It's beautiful! Beats anything was ever painted on a book cover.'

'All I know is it's damn cold!' Augie rasped as the Concord gained the level ground through a rock-strewn pass. He yelled at the team and cracked the reins. The horses responded eagerly to the command for speed. 'Beats me why folks want to come up to this godforsaken place to listen to a fiddle player!'

'Rollo Stone is the greatest violinist in the world,' Hiram argued, reverting to his cultured New York accent. 'And he composes all his own pieces. People go wild about him. Especially the women. And there are going to be others at High Mountain. The Alice Cooper Choir and Robert Dillon, the famous baritone. As well as the Jefferson Surrey Orchestra. Lots of other famous musicians, too. Why, it's going to be the finest festival of music ever staged.'

Edge glanced over his shoulder and saw that Hiram had donned a warm coat that completely covered him from neck to ankles as he sat cross-legged on the swaying roof of the Concord. It was buttoned to the throat and its fur collar was turned up. The white ten-gallon hat, stained by mud and somebody's blood, looked incongruous atop his youthful face.

The youngster seemed to be embarrassed by the half-breed's empty gaze and showed a nervous grin. There was not a hint in his appearance or manner that he had recently murdered two helpless men. 'I like music almost as much as reading,' he explained, making it sound like an excuse.

'Supposed to be better for kids than hanging around poolrooms,' Edge allowed sardonically.

'There she is, folks!' Augie yelled with audible relief. 'End of the line.'

The half-breed swung his head around to face front as the coach sped through the pass and its bulky driver hauled on the reins to slow the team for a tight curve on the other side. Heads were thrust from windows to catch a first glimpse of the Concord's destination.

Far below, close to the bottom of a great dish scooped in the mountains, the lights of a town burned bright and unflickering through the clear night air. The lights gleamed in two parallel rows to mark out the line of a single street, at the western end of which was a far broader area of bright illumination. The softer glow of the moon augmented the lamp light.

The street ran in a straight line from east to west along the southern rim of a deep chasm that sank to the lowest point in the great circular basin amid the peaks. The buildings on either side of the broad thoroughfare were a mixture of single and double storey, of timber, redbrick and local stone; with covered sidewalks running along the front of the buildings, broken at the alleys which gave on to back lots.

From the terraced crop fields that were spread to the south

42

and the sloping pastureland extending up the northern side of the basin beyond the chasm, it was apparent that High Mountain was a farming community. The kind that, under normal circumstances, would have been dark and quiet at such a late hour.

But the circumstance of a music festival was not normal and as the Concord drew nearer – at first inching around dangerous hairpin curves and then making speed down a shallow grade between the well-tended fields – those aboard were able to hear the noise that accompanied the bright lights. Music, laughter, loud voices, the thud of feet against floorboards and the general background hum of a wide-open town provided a raucous contrast to the almost awesome silence clamped over the surrounding peaks.

'Hot damn!' Augie snarled, hauling on the reins to bring the team to a walk. 'Not more friggin' trouble here!'

His outburst was caused by a line of four men who had appeared to block the way. They emerged from the moon shadow of a two-storey brick building at the point where the trail ran out to become the eastern end of the street. All were tall, all carried a lot of solid weight and all moved with the smooth ease of youth. They were dressed entirely in black, from highly sheened boots to the low crowns of their hats. Their jackets and pants were of shiny buckskin, the coats hiked up at the right hip to show the jutting butts of holstered revolvers.

The quartet stood immobile in the path of the slowing Concord, mere silhouettes against the lights of the street stretched out behind them.

'Hey, you could get run down doin' somethin' like that!' the weary Augie snarled in exasperation as he halted the team, the lead pair only a few feet from the men.

'Welcome to the High Mountain Festival of Fine Music,' the one who had led the others across the street announced flatly. 'Ben Tallis says we gotta check you ain't bringin' no trouble here.'

He sounded bored by the words, as if he had made the same short speech a thousand times. Glancing along the crowded sidewalks and at the mass of people milling around the brightly lit tented area at the far end of the street, Edge guessed it might have been that many.

'Oh, Jesus,' Augie hissed so that only the half-breed could hear. 'The Devil's Disciples!'

'We're bringing trouble aplenty!' Hiram announced.

Hands rose fast to drape four gun butts.

'Don't draw those irons!' Hiram warned.

'Trouble to bury, is all!' Augie put in hurriedly, the nervous tic starting up in his right cheek.

'After we been paid bounty on it!' Hiram augmented. 'We was bushwacked by four varmints.'

Edge glanced over his shoulder. Hiram was standing upright between the two tightly-wrapped corpses. He had unbuttoned his long coat to reveal his entire rhinestone-studded garb.

The news failed to interest the four gunmen and they were unmoved by the outlandishly attired youngster.

'We only got jurisdiction up to the rim,' their spokesman announced. He waved his free hand in a circular motion to indicate the high limit of the basin. 'Didn't happen local or we'd have heard it. Need to see all your folks got festival tickets. Or stage line credentials.'

He stepped forward as the Baron leaned from the window, his bewhiskered face set in a glower. 'Who are you, sir?' he demanded. 'To delay us after such a distressing and arduous journey?'

'Wants to see your tickets, folks,' Augie supplied, still afraid of the black-garbed quartet. 'One of the fellers hired to help out the local law.'

He handed down confirmation of his identity and Hiram extended a piece of pasteboard.

'Very well,' the Baron submitted stiffly, and turned his head to peer back into the coach. 'It is all right, my friends. The fellow is merely doing his job.'

The Englishman thrust a handful of tickets through the window and these were examined closely, together with that from the kid and Augie's letter. Then the man pushed the whole bundle back at the Baron.

'Okay,' he growled in the same flat tone, shooting a dull-eyed glance at the undraped bodies slumped across the horses in back of the Concord. 'But keep this rig off the street until you unload the stiffs. Law office and mortician's place are on that side. We don't want nice folks upset, get me?'

His eyes glinted with a warning for a moment, then he backed away and returned to take his place at the end of the blocking line.

'Mean-looking critters, aren't they?' Hiram murmured.

44

'Real mean,' Augie hissed as he urged the team into movement and steered the Concord towards the rear of the buildings lining the north side of the street. 'Run up against them once before. Bunch of trigger happy vigilantes that Ben Tallis hires out for big money. Work California mostly. And if you have the lousy luck to run in with Tallis, you'll know why he calls 'em Devil's Disciples.'

They were behind the buildings now, out of earshot of the hired guns. And Augie suddenly cackled with laughter. 'Mean as fellers get to be,' he rasped. 'But real dumb.'

'Letter covered Luke and you both, uh?' Edge suggested.

'Sure did,' the driver responded. 'But they never figured you weren't Luke.'

'Obliged,' the half-breed acknowledged.

'My pleasure, mister,' Augie assured, his laughter subsiding to a grin of satisfaction. 'Never thought I'd see the day I'd fool a Tallis man.'

Edge expressed a subtler brand of humour that was just an upturn at the corners of his mouth. 'Should have known it would work like a charm.'

Chapter Five

THE law office was at a midway point along the north side of the street – a stone building just one storey high with a cell block at the rear. It was tacked on, seemingly as an afterthought, at the end of a two-storey block comprised of the stage depot, town bank, hardware store and a restaurant called The Big Basin. Across an alley, wide enough to take the Concord, was a wood-built church with a high steeple.

Edge blinked against the bright lights of the street as he stepped from the half-darkness of the alley.

'Guess this is what's called riproaring,' Hiram said with high excitement as he halted alongside the half-breed.

He had scrambled down from the coach roof immediately behind Edge, but then had held back to shed his long coat and to dust off the dried mud from his highly decorated outfit.

'When it ain't called fleecing the suckers,' Edge replied, ignoring the looks of curiosity, disgust and even scorn which were directed by the passersby at himself and Hiram.

Windows in almost every building along both sides of the street were ablaze with yellow lamplight; hung adjacent to the majority of them were hurriedly painted signs proclaiming a brand of goods or type of service offered by the owners. These in addition to the premises which continued their normal lines of business – the restaurant, the Peaks Saloon and Hotel, O'Leary's Dry Goods Store, Bartholomew's Poolroom and a handful of others catering to the everyday needs of a small town. Elsewhere, *Rooms* signs were displayed in a score of places. Advertisements for *Take-Away Liquor* were almost as numerous. A palmist operated from a private house. A twenty-four hour fire kindling and lamp oil service was offered by the hardware store. And the town doctor had covered his normal shingle with a sign which claimed he ran an infirmary; another sign under a blazing window across the street maintained that Grout's Snake Medicine would cure all human ailments. Games of chance were offered in a dozen places, there was a polka dance in the meeting hall, religious carvings were on sale from the church and food – from popcorn to exotic foreign delicacies – could be purchased from pushcarts and open windows.

Business was booming everywhere, as well-dressed visitors to the town moved in and out of brightly lit doorways, between times strolling the sidewalks or criss-crossing the street which was hung with coloured lanterns and strung with banners proclaiming the reason for the excitement: *The High Mountain Festival of Fine Music.*

'Reckon there ain't nothing that's cheap to be had in this one-horse town right now,' Hiram allowed, hitching up his gunbelt.

As the half-breed and the kid stepped up on to the sidewalk fronting the law office and Augie helped his passengers out of the Concord, it was obvious why the newcomers drew passing attention away from the town's long-established and new enterprises. For their travel-stained appearance and weary features were at complete odds with the fine attire and clean faces of the men and women thronging the street. Most of them looking as rich as Edge's fellow-passengers, displaying their wealth by the cut of their clothes and the sparkle of their jewellery.

But in such a crowd of mainly elderly, obvious city dwellers, a few others stood out as noticeably as the recent arrivals. These were the black-garbed Tallis men, similar in age and identical in appearance to the quartet who had halted the Concord at the town limits. They prowled the sidewalks or lounged against building façades, their guns displayed from hiked up jackets and their eyes constantly raking over the ever-moving tableau of rich folks on the hoof. As one of the men did a slow turn, to gaze insolently at a middle-aged but

47

beautiful woman, the stud-formed lettering on the back of his sheened jacket reflected the lights: *Devil's Disciple – California.*

'This Tallis critter sure seems to have a lot of help,' Hiram said as Edge reached the law office doorway and took a final look around as he fisted a hand over the knob.

'Hell of a lot,' the half-breed said evenly as he pushed open the door and stepped across the threshold.

'Shut that goddamn door on that goddamn Sodom and Gommorah out there!' the man behind the desk yelled from under his hat.

The desk was at the rear of the room, to one side of another door that gave on to the cell block. It was a large desk bearing just a clean blotter, a lamp with the wick turned low, and two empty wooden trays. The man in the swivel chair behind the desk was also large. Not so much in girth, though he probably weighed better than two hundred and fifty pounds, but he had the height to carry it without slack for he was close to seven feet tall. His chair was turned slightly sideways-on to the desk, so that he could rest his long legs at full stretch on the uncluttered top. His elbows were braced on the chair arms and his chin was propped on clasped fingers. His face was completely hidden by his hat.

'Hell, he's a big critter!' Hiram gasped as he closed the door.

Because of the stout stone walls of the office, the din outside suddenly seemed to come from a great distance.

'Name's Fyson,' the sheriff supplied, unbunching a fist and pushing the hat onto the back of his head. 'Near enough to seven feet as makes no difference. On account of which I get called High Fy.'

'Wow!' Hiram exclaimed, his eyes raking along the length of the lawman again. 'Seven feet – that's just got to be a record of some kind.'

'He sure don't look like a stereotype,' the half-breed said.

Sheriff Fyson was about forty with deeply bronzed features that might have been modelled from a mountain crag, with the eyes representing dark lakes between snow-fringed shores. The structure was angular and the skin was pitted and cracked. But there was a certain rugged handsomeness to the face, which showed an expression of dislike as the dark eyes surveyed the newcomers.

He had a five-pointed tin star pinned to the left pocket of

his checked shirt. His pants were blue levis, the cuffs tucked into his boot tops. A single-holster gunbelt was hung around his hips. The loops were fully stocked with shells and the holster carried an old Remington .44 Army Model.

'Something I can do for you, cousins?' he asked, his voice a lazy Southern drawl. His eyes remained unfriendly.

'Six corpses outside in the alley,' Edge said, moving to a pot-bellied stove that stood against one wall alongside a rack of six Winchesters.

The lawman's eyes were abruptly more unfriendly and he dragged his legs off the desk and slammed his feet to the floor. 'I sure do hope you're trying to make a joke of some kind, cousin!' he warned.

'We were bushwhacked, Sheriff!' Hiram supplied quickly, jerking out of his fascinated appraisal of the lanky lawman. 'Four of the varmints. All of them riding the range in the sky now. Lost a couple of our own, though.'

Edge had wedged the Winchester between his knees and was standing with his back to the warmth of the stove, his hands splayed in line with the heat. Fyson's unblinking eyes raked a scornful gaze up and down the kid, then swung to look at the half-breed.

'It ain't no joke, is it?' he asked with a sigh. 'Even them pretty threads the kid's wearing don't make it no goddamn joke, does it, cousin?'

Edge shook his head. 'Hiram's learning as he goes along. Some things faster than others.'

'I saw off two of them,' the kid boasted, unconcerned by Fyson's blatantly contemptuous attitude towards him. 'Edge here gave the other two their tickets to Boot Hill.' He hitched up his gunbelt. 'My name's Rydell. Kid Rydell.'

'Kid Rydell?' Edge rasped.

'It's gotta be better than Hiram or Junior,' the youngster pointed out evenly.

The sheriff raised his hat to scratch at his thick growth of greying red hair. 'Gave them their what to where?' he asked.

'Killed them is all,' Edge explained with a sigh. 'Hiram read a lot of books back East about the West. You want to check if the dead are worth anything except burying?'

'Where'd it happen?'

'In the mountains. South.'

'A long ways from here, Sheriff,' Hiram added.

4   49

Fyson got wearily to his feet and had to hunch his shoulders to keep from hitting his head on the ceiling. 'Four you say?' he asked from the door.

'Two notches each for our guns,' Hiram confirmed.

'Could be the Warner bunch. Ran them boys outta High Mountain before the Tallis vigilantes took over the law business here. They rode south.'

The noise of the town crowded into the office for a moment, then the door closed behind the lawman.

'He's a critter rides tall in the saddle, ain't he?' the kid muttered, and took the time to gaze around the office with as much fascination as he showed for each new scene or person he came upon. 'And he's got the same kinda eyes as you. Filled with far horizons.'

'Hiram?'

'Yeah, Edge?'

'One day you're going to call the wrong feller critter.'

The kid nodded and pursed his lips. 'Got you, Edge.'

Time crawled slowly in the warm, dimy lit office, the passing seconds marked by the loud tick of a wall clock. Edge continued to stand before the stove while Hiram opened the door in the rear wall. He grunted with disappointment when he saw that the two cells were vacant.

'I was right, cousins,' the lawman drawled when he returned to the office and closed the door gratefully behind him. 'Flyers out on them from Santa Fe. Bank robbing. Don't say whether dead or alive, but I guess it don't make no difference. Hundred bucks apiece to anyone without a badge.' He went towards a safe at one side of the only window and used a key from a ring hung on his belt. 'Worth only trouble to a lawman, which is why I just contented myself running them out.'

'A hundred each!' the beaming Hiram exclaimed. 'Well, I'll be.'

'Just remember about critters,' Edge warned. 'Or could be you won't be much longer, Hiram.'

'Don't mind Edge calling me Hiram,' the kid told Fyson as the safe door swung open. 'On account we been through a mess of trouble together.'

'I saw and heard about it, cousin,' the lawman answered. 'Harv Danby – town's mortician – is taking care of the arrangements. The Warner bunch and passenger and shotgun. Hold-up happened outside my jurisdiction so I just pay you fellers and that's it as far as I'm concerned.'

He counted out the bills as he spoke, then gave one stack to the kid and one to Edge. All in twenties and fives.

'Hey, I'm twenty bucks short,' Hiram complained after checking his money while Fyson returned to his relaxed posture in the swivel chair.

'You pay to bury the men you kill, Hiram,' Edge told him, pocketing his share of the bounty without counting it. Then he canted the rifle to his shoulder. 'Obliged to you, Sheriff.'

The lawman had his feet back up on the desk and the hat tipped forward over his face again. 'Santa Fe marshal's office foots the bill. No skin off my nose. But don't you fellers get trigger happy on my patch.'

'You said the Devil's Disciples are running the law around here now,' Hiram pointed out, clutching what was probably the first money he had ever earned in his life.

'Suits me to let them think they do, cousin,' Fyson answered. 'Long as they stop trouble happening. Soon as it does, the troublemakers'll answer to me.'

'I'm just here for the music, Sheriff,' Hiram said.

'Ain't you I'm anxious about, sonny,' the lawman countered and raised his hat a fraction to fix Edge with a steel-eyed gaze.

'No sweat from me, feller,' the half-breed told him. 'Heard from a drummer down in Arizona there was a shindig due here. Aim to find me a room and an honest poker game.'

'Neither'd be a problem any other time, cousin. But don't you start no ruckus when you can't get either of them after a long trip like you've had.'

'Nothing worthwhile's easy, feller,' Edge replied, and stepped outside.

In the shelter of the basin, the temperature was a good deal higher than it had been up among the peaks. But, by contrast to the cosy warmth of the law office, the outside air seemed to be threaded with tendrils of ice.

'Reckon I'll mosey down to the mortician's office,' Hiram said, his youthful features forming into an expression of remembered grief. 'I wanna make sure Aunt Emma don't have no ten dollar planting in Potter's Field.'

Edge nodded. 'You and her have rooms booked?'

'Dang it, that's right! She won't be needing no bed now, will she?' He grinned his pleasure at the prospect of being able to help the half-breed. 'The Houston Music Society got in early. There's some rooms for us at the hotel. Most folks only got boarding houses or having to sleep under canvas.'

He jerked a thumb along the street towards the tent town at the eastern end of High Mountain.

'Obliged, Hiram.'

'See you in the saloon for a brew, maybe?'

The kid hurried off along the crowded street and Edge swung down from the sidewalk and turned into the alley. The Concord was still parked where it had halted. The passengers had dispersed and the corpses and baggage had been removed. But the team was still in the traces and the four saddle horses remained hitched to the rear of the coach. The short and overweight Augie was making a sales pitch to a tall, thin, bald-headed man in dungarees.

'The Sheriff says you and the kid earned yourselves some bounty money,' the stage driver said quickly as Edge approached. The nervous tic was moving his cheek again.

'High Fy ain't concerned with our dealin's,' the horse-trader whined. 'Twenty-five bucks apiece, take it or leave it. You keep the saddles and stuff. Get a better price elsewhere. But ain't no elsewhere closer than twenty miles to here.'

He spat.

Augie shuffled his feet and rasped a hand over his jaw bristles. 'Well, I ain't rightly sure the nags are mine to sell.'

'This one ain't, feller,' Edge said evenly, unhitching the grey hollow back he had selected when he first found the horses.

'You figure the kid'll lay claim to the others, Mr Edge?' Augie asked anxiously.

'I hear he's getting to talk like me,' the half-breed answered, unbuckling the cinch and letting the saddle and bedroll fall to the ground. 'But that don't mean I can speak for him.'

He stepped up on to a coach wheel to drag his own gear off the roof. He draped it across the back of the gelding without fastening it and led the horse out of the alley.

'Well, where is he so I can ask him?' Augie yelled as the horse-trader grew impatient to close the deal.

Edge jerked a thumb towards the western end of the street. 'Guess he'd like me to tell you he went thataway!'

'Hey, you!' a man roared across the din of the town as Edge started to move towards the De Cruz Livery Stables. 'Get that horse off the street.'

The press of evening strollers and pleasure seekers had opened up a gap for the half-breed to take his mount from one side of the street to the other. Abruptly, another corridor was driven through the crowd from a different direction as two of the Devil's Disciples shoved and elbowed their way towards Edge.

'No animals allowed on the street while the festival's on.'

'Exceptin' for ours.'

The two black-garbed gunmen had been stationed on either side of the batswing doors of the saloon, directly across from the law office. The livery was fifty yards further west along the street, beyond a crowded millinery store and the music-filled meeting hall. The two Tallis men skidded to a halt ten paces in front of Edge, when he was still twenty yards short of his objective.

'People want to get animals from one side of the street to the other, they gotta take them around town,' the man on the left snarled. He had a thin moustache along his top lip and a dimple on his chin. 'Didn't you know that?'

Edge had halted when the two men moved into the open area. His tone was as nonchalant as his stance. 'Heard that was just when there were dead men across the horses.'

The one on the right shook his head. He was clean-shaven and had cut himself during his most recent effort to stay that way. 'It's on account Mr Box don't want people walkin' through horse droopin's. He knows it now, Joe.' He pointed a finger and made a circular motion in the air. 'So why don't you turn around and do like you're supposed to, mister?'

Edge glanced briefly over his shoulder, and spotted a third gunman moving out of the alley between the law office and the church. 'I figure I got less ground to cover if I keep going ahead,' he answered evenly as he looked at the men again.

Beyond them, he glimpsed two familiar forms. The Baron was in the saloon doorway, sucking slowly from a glass. Hiram Rydell was watching from the sidewalk in front of the mortician's black-velvet draped window.

The mouthlines of the gunmen tightened and their bodies became rigid. Hands moved fractionally towards jutting Colt butts. Many of the bystanders moved hurriedly away. While others jostled to get a clearer view of what was happening.

'Don't tangle with them bastards, mister!' a woman rasped from behind Edge, to the left.

The half-breed sighed. 'Be obliged you fellers didn't draw those guns on me. Give folks just the one warning about that.'

'Tough talk won't get you nowhere,' Joe growled. 'We got word from Mr Box personal we can use force to see the festival rules get obeyed.'

'He got the same rules for blood as for horseshit?' Edge asked.

Some women gasped. Perhaps at the prospect of violence – or maybe at the sound of bad language.

'We sure have got us a tough nut, Harry.' The dimple on Joe's chin deepened when he smiled.

'Seems like, Joe. Let's crack him, uh?'

The distance between Edge and the gunmen made a lunge impossible. His left hand held the gelding's reins and his right kept the Winchester canted to his shoulder. The rifle was un-cocked. He remained motionless, narrowed eyes flicking from one gunman to the other. A blanket of tense silence fell over the area of the street where two men faced a third. Beyond, the town was as noisy as ever but the sounds of merriment and hard-selling seemed to be carried only outwards from the centre of High Mountain.

'A final chance, feller!' Joe snarled. 'Back up!'

They drew in unison. Fast and smooth: both hammers cocked and the muzzles aimed unwaveringly at the half-breed's heart.

'Just do as you're told, tough nut!' Harry ordered. 'Kill you if you don't. And we got the law on our side. Been deputised.'

Still grinning, Joe flipped up a lapel of his coat to display a tin star.

Only the look in the half-breed's unblinking eyes hinted that the casual attitude was a deception. But they were mere glint-ing threads of blue in the shadow of his hat brim and a man would have to be very close to read what was behind those hooded eyes. There was fear there, and a brand of tension that used fear as a weapon. A long time ago, at the outset of the War Between the States, he had been afraid only of killing. Then, as one bloody battle followed another, the young cavalry officer underwent an involuntary reversal: to slaughter and maim the enemy while in the grip of a searing sense of exhilara-tion that scorched all other emotions into extinction. Acting with the same degree of recklessness as Hiram back at the gorge.

But then he had come to recognise fear as an essential pre-requisite of survival – provided it was a kind of fear that was as ice cold and controlled as the exhilaration had been white hot and mindless. The kind that kept a man's senses sharp and allowed his brain to function positively while his reflexes were poised for smooth action. Thus, behind the hard eyes and casual stance, Edge was as aware of the cold grip of such fear as he was of every other aspect of his readiness to combat this new danger.

'Seems I have to turn around and go back,' he said evenly.

Now both Devil's Disciples grinned. And Harry displayed his beaming face to the watchers on either side as Edge started to turn the gelding. Some of the bystanders nodded approvingly while others glared at the half-breed with blatant scorn. On one side of the street, Hiram expressed disappointment and the Baron watched with avid interest: still drinking steadily. On the other side, the towering lawman divided his attention between Edge and the black-garbed gunman at the mouth of the alley. His craggy face alternately showed mild approval and grim warning.

The half-breed kept his movements slow, backing to stand beside the horse, then tugging gently on the reins to ease the animal around. When the horse was between himself and the gunmen on the street, he powered into speed.

He sprang open his hand on the Winchester and the rifle started to slide off his shoulder. His lean face retained its calm set – and his hand streaked to snatch at the butt of his holstered Colt. But the move was hidden from the gunmen by the gelding. They merely added a twist of contempt to their grins, see-ing the dropped rifle as a sign of nervous clumsiness – until the Winchester hit the ground and Edge powered down on to his haunches.

'Watch him!' the man from the alley roared.

Edge heard the warning, and the gasps, screams and yells that exploded from a score of throats to either side of him.

Then the Colt bucked in his hand. Joe staggered backwards, a gush of blood arcing from the centre of his forehead. He was still grinning when the bullet drilled into his brain.

Harry had time to form his features into a snarl of hatred. He saw the glinting-eyed face of Edge looking at him from under the belly of the gelding, but the half-breed's gun cracked a second time before Harry could track his Colt low enough.

And it was Edge who grinned now, curling back his lips to show the line where his teeth were clenched: as Harry took a bullet in the heart.

The open area of the street had widened to twice its size since Joe went down. Now Harry started to corkscrew to the ground, and his finger squeezed the trigger an instant before he died. The bullet spun across ten yards of cold night air and drove into the flank of the gelding.

Edge whirled in the crouch – and stayed his trigger finger. For the gunman in the alley was held in rigid inertia: as if pinned to the spot by an extension from the aimed barrel of Fyson's Remington.

The pool of silence extended much further after the explosion of shots: tense and brittle for stretched seconds as it waited to be shattered.

'Was self-defence, cousin,' the tall lawman drawled.

The horse's forelegs buckled. A woman screamed and the gelding snorted. Countless throats roared a reaction to violence. Edge snatched up his Winchester, half-turned, and powered out of the crouch. Then vented a snarl as, for the second time that day, he scrambled from under the crushing weight of a wounded horse.

The gelding kept his hindlegs rigid until he canted on to a shoulder and rolled on to his side. Then he lashed all four legs as he tried to turn and bite at the wound.

The silence came back – to grip the entire town now. Deeper, harder and more tense than anything which had preceded it. Attention, directed from faces etched with shock, fear or excitement, switched from Edge, to the horse, to the bodies, to the lawman and back around the same route again.

'Things ain't always what they seem,' the half-breed muttered.

Then he slid the Colt into his holster and pumped the action of the Winchester as he threw the stock to his shoulder. The gelding gave up trying to reach the source of his agony and his head slammed to the ground. The rifle exploded a shot from a range of five feet. The bullet went into horseflesh behind the ear and the gelding twitched once and was still.

From many directions, grim-faced Devil's Disciples converged towards the centre of violence.

'Tallis was warned, goddamn it!' Fyson roared. 'He won't goddamn like this!'

Edge pumped the rifle action and did a slow turn, the stock still against his shoulder. The crowd drew back further, those at the front leaning hard against those at the rear. Like robots, the black-garbed figures came to a halt. Ten of them at least. Maybe more. Hatred etched deep into the lines of their hard, mean faces.

'Sokalski, what do we do?' one of them yelled.

There was a short pause. Then: 'Boss'll be here soon. Feller'll keep until then.'

Edge turned but didn't see Sokalski's face. Just the broad back, with the studded lettering on the sheen surface of the black buckskin jacket as the man moved away through the crowd.

'Warned you people there'd be killing!' Fyson roared. And holstered his revolver.

A honky-tonk piano and a fiddle started to make off-key music in the saloon. A larger group of entertainers began a different tune in the meeting hall. Hands and feet beat time and men yelled for drinks. A woman shrieked with laughter. The crowds on the street stirred into movement again. The noise swelled to the volume it had held before the gunfight. The strolling resumed its former cadence. But now, the death-strewn, blood-run area of street in front of the meeting hall was regarded as a no-man's land.

'Guess you didn't need no advice,' a woman said as Edge eased the Winchester's hammer to the rest and canted the rifle to his shoulder. He recognised the voice as the same one which had hissed the warning to him.

She was a slender redhead with green eyes who might have been pretty had her teeth not been so prominent. She looked about thirty, but it was possible she could be several years younger under the thick layer of make-up pancaked on her face. Her dress picked up the colour of her eyes, but was far newer and did not yet show so many signs of ill-used experience. It was cut low to reveal all her shoulders and much of her breasts, fitted skin tight to the waist to contour the curves of her torso. Her hair was held in a bun on top of her head. Her smile was part admiration and part invitation.

'I work in the saloon if you need some relaxation after the excitement, mister.' Her backward glance was a mockery of coyness as she started towards the batswings. 'Name's Virginia – and no cracks.'

Edge stooped to recover his fallen gear. He looked up and the line of his mouth came as close as it ever did to expressing warm humour. 'So how d'you make a living?' he asked.

Chapter Six

THE man who emerged from the undertaking parlour was short and slightly built, about fifty, with a ring of grey hair surrounding his bald skull. He had wizened features that seemed to be set in a permanent expression of resignation.

He hurried to the bodies, crouched between them and vented a grunt of satisfaction. 'They're mine, Mr Fyson. Dead as all get out.'

'Mighty fine shooting, Edge,' Hiram congratulated with a broad smile as he emerged from the crowd, on the other side of the open area from the lawman. 'Knew you could handle it, so I just stayed watching.'

'Told you Hiram learns some things fast,' the half-breed growled at Fyson.

'You ain't no slouch yourself, cousin,' the sheriff muttered. Then, to Harv Danby. 'Get the mess off the street. All three of the animals. Tallis'll pay burying expenses.'

'Ain't you going to pay, Edge?' Hiram asked.

'That's only when there's bounty money on the dead,' the half-breed explained, as he met the piercing gaze of Fyson.

'You caught my drift about trouble, cousin. Don't concern me none if every Tallis man in town gets blasted. Long as the fighting's fair.'

'Fifty bucks'll buy you a fast ride outta High Mountain, mister!' This from the dungareed horse-trader who had emerged from the alley beside the law office, an avaricious smile pasted to his face beneath his bald dome. He jerked a thumb over his shoulder.

'I told Augie he could have the horses to sell, Edge,' Hiram said.

'Buy one and beat it,' Fyson advised. 'You just started a war with the Tallis bunch and they ain't the peace treatying kind, cousin. Soon as Tallis gets here, all hell's going to cut loose. Innocent people are liable to get hurt. That happens, I'll see everyone responsible pays for it. Guess I don't have to paint it no clearer than that, cousin? Not a man gets my drift easy as you do?'

'Your meaning's as plain to see as you are, Sheriff,' Edge allowed, then glanced at the horse-trader. 'Later, feller.'

'There ain't much later left for him,' a man snarled from out of the crowd on one side.

'And he don't wanna waste fifty bucks on somethin' he won't get to use,' another voice taunted from elsewhere.

Fyson turned and started back towards his office. Hiram snapped his head from side to side, to glare into the hard-set faces of the watching Tallis men. When he looked back at Edge, the half-breed had stepped around the horse carcase and was heading for the saloon entrance. The young New Yorker, spurs jingling, ran to catch up.

'High Fy's right, Edge,' he said excitedly. 'I reckon you're gonna have to have a showdown with the whole bunch of critters. You want me to back your play?'

The half-breed halted with one foot on the sidewalk: and turned his head to fix the youngster with a scornful stare. 'Want you to just back off from me, Hiram,' he answered coldly.

A hurt expression spread fast across the fuzzed, baby-faced handsomeness of the kid's features. Then, as he saw the full depth of the half-breed's brooding anger, he swallowed hard and licked his lips. But he was quick to control his fear. 'All right, mister!' he snapped. 'You don't have to make no smoke signals. But you weren't so damn independent when we got held up, doggone it!'

He stared into Edge's lean face for a moment longer. And, in that brief segment of time, fear was totally replaced by bitterness. Then he whirled and forced a way through the press of the crowd.

Edge vented a low sigh and stepped up on to the sidewalk.

'Sir, I think that is the first decent thing you have done in a very long time!'

The Baron stood on the threshold of the saloon, a brimful glass of whiskey in one hand while the other was fisted around his stick, holding open one of the batswings. His bewhiskered face glowed crimson with the liquor that was already coursing through his bloodstream.

'You will allow me to buy you a drink – to mark such an auspicious occasion, sir?' he added as Edge stepped through the open door.

'Obliged for the offer, feller,' the half-breed answered, feeling the tautness drain out of his body and the stiffness go from his facial muscles. 'But I'm up to my neck in favours already.'

'You will, of course, purchase a drink for me in return, sir,' the Englishman insisted. 'Nothing lost and nothing gained. A little relaxation while you contemplate how to extricate yourself from this dangerous situation.'

Edge halted just across the threshold and glanced impassively over the smoke-laden, noise-filled, malodorous saloon. Many of the patrons eyed him fleetingly and then quickly returned to what had interested them before his entrance. Two Devil's Disciples at a table near the foot of the stairway glared at him with heavy menace.

The slitted eyes of the half-breed showed a flicker of interest only twice – when he spotted two poker games where the pots were encouragingly large.

'What's the point, feller?' he asked.

The Baron blinked. 'Point, sir?'

'If there's nothing to lose and nothing to gain?'

The Englishman shook his head in time with the flapping of the batswing door after he had released it behind Edge. 'Sir, such a degree of bitterness saddens me greatly,' he answered, then raised his glass and emptied its contents down his throat at a gulp. He swayed and had to use his cane to keep himself from falling. 'I find it painful to watch – '

'You ain't feeling no pain, feller,' Edge told him evenly, and started towards the bar.

The hard eyes of the two Devil's Disciples followed him like those of preying animals watching for the right moment to spring to the attack.

'You ain't gonna cause no trouble in my places are you, mister?' the anxious sweaty-faced owner of the Peaks Saloon and Hotel asked as his new customer bellied up to the bar.

Edge dropped his gear to the floor and leaned the Winchester against the front panel of the counter. He rasped the back of a hand over his jaw bristles and looked away from the nervous, slightly built, middle-aged man who smelled of sweat oozing from pores elsewhere than on his face and neck.

'You'll have to tell me,' the half-breed said, running his gaze over a banner that was strung along the wall above the shelves of bottles and glasses.

'Tell you what?'

'Rules of the house so I'll know what not to do. Whiskey and a beer to help me digest them?'

'Comin' right up. Only rules are against gunplay and fist fights. And no credit. Pay for what you get when you get it.'

Edge nodded as the glasses were set on the bar and filled. He put down a five dollar bill. 'Always pay my way.'

He glanced away from the banner for just long enough to tip the whiskey in the beer and pick up his change.

'That all?'

'You've got a room for rent.'

'No, sir. Right filled up.'

'Woman from Houston reserved one. Mortician's arranging things for her now.'

The owner shook his head. 'Sorry,' he said, and didn't look it. 'I heard what happened out on the trail. Already rented the room. To another lady.'

He drew Edge's attention away from the banner again, and pointed towards the stairway which led up a side wall of the saloon towards a railed balcony. The red-headed Virginia was descending through the smoke haze, trailed by a grinning young man in a cutaway coat who was still tucking his shirt tails in his pants.

'That's a lady?'

'In a manner of speakin', mister.'

'Prefer truth to manners, feller. I'd say she's a whore.'

The man behind the bar shrugged. 'Have it your way.'

'Not with a whore. Obliged anyway.'

He resumed his study of the banner and the saloon owner

moved to help out his three bartenders who were losing ground in meeting the demands of patrons for refills.

Like most of the other advertisements around town concerned with the musical event and its connected money-making activities, this one was of grey canvas lettered in red. And, in common with the others produced by the organisers of the main attraction, it seemed to have been painted by a professional sign-writer:

Not to be missed
The High Mountain Festival of Fine Music
with
Direct from New York
The Rollo Stone Ensemble
Plus a full programme of talented supporting artistes
from every corner of the musical world. Three days
of unparalleled musical entertainment performed in a
scenic setting of Mother Nature's design.

Beneath this main announcement were several columns listing the singers, musicians and dancers of lesser note than the big attraction. Those Hiram had spoken of, and many more.

'You don't look the type, mister,' Virginia said lightly, moving up close to Edge as he scanned the listing – and was not surprised the names meant nothing to him.

'What type's that, ma'am?'

'The type that has fun sittin' and listenin' to high-brow fiddle players, singers and such like.'

Edge had filled time reading every name on the list. He eyed the whore with the same lack of interest.

'Why, I bet you never heard of any of them,' she challenged with a bright smile, waving a hand at the banner. Her fingernails were as bright red as her painted lips. Oddly, the more she smiled, the further her full lips closed to encroach over her teeth. And she became almost pretty.

'Once knew a guy named . . . ' He glanced up at the sign again ' . . . Campbell. Back in the war. Picked guitar a little. Always talking about Galveston.'

'Not the same one. This guy plays harp.'

'Guess not,' Edge allowed lightly. 'Feller I knew was heading for Kansas. Planned to get a job with the telegraph company working out of Wichita.'

63

'*I* work here, remember? Ten dollars a trick, but you get a discount for bumping off them two Tallis creeps.'

The half-breed finished the drink and picked up his gear and rifle.

'Whores and ladies,' the saloon owner said cheerfully as he retrieved Edge's empty glass. He grinned. 'They all got the kinda medicine a man needs when he needs it, right?'

'Just a matter of whether a feller wants to risk a dose,' the half-breed muttered, and turned to follow Virginia towards the foot of the stairway.

'Have a good time,' one of the black-garbed Devil's Disciples snarled from where he sat at the table playing solitaire. He didn't glance up from the cards.

His partner was picking at his teeth with a split match. 'Yeah, and maybe if you're still screwing her when Mr Tallis hits town, could be you'll die happy.'

'It's okay, Mr Edge,' the whore said quickly, staring hatefully at the two gunmen. 'I got no honour needs defendin'.'

'Guess you'll still be around when I'm ready for you, fellers?' Edge asked evenly.

'You're bettin' your life on it, mister,' the card-player growled.

As Edge trailed the whore up the stairway, he glimpsed the Baron leaning heavily against one end of the bar, glaring disgust through the liquor sheen of his eyes. Then the half-breed glanced towards the batswings in time to see Hiram Rydell swagger into the saloon and peer searchingly around. But the youngster failed to spot the couple on the stairway through the swirl of tobacco smoke. He made a bee-line towards the drunken Englishman.

The railed balcony extended around all four sides of the saloon, with room doors set into the wall at twenty feet intervals. When the whore halted and pushed open a door, Edge gestured with the rifle for her to go in ahead of him.

'Not because you're a gentleman, I guess?' she said goodhumouredly.

'I don't have to guess about you not being a lady,' he replied.

Her line of work had given her a thick skin beneath the paint and powder and she swayed into the room with her good mood still intact. Then halted at the centre to twirl and face him, her arms out wide.

'Ain't no one in here but this chicken, Mr Edge,' she chided.

Then grinned: 'Okay, I ain't no chicken either.'

Edge stepped across the threshold and used the stock of his rifle to close the door. The only light came from the lanterns strung above the street beyond the single small window. It was enough to show the shapes of a double bed, a mirrored-dresser, a chair, the door to a closet and two rush mats. The walls were white painted timber with magazine pictures pasted on them here and there. There was a lamp on the dresser, its oil smell competing with the whore's perfume and a stronger odour of stale cigar smoke.

'You want me to light the lamp?' Virginia asked.

'Everything you got where it's supposed to be?' Edge countered as he moved to the uncurtained window and looked down into the street.

'You don't want no light,' she acknowledged with a nod, and reached behind her back for the dress fastenings. 'Eight bucks okay? Two dollars discount ain't much, but then that scum you killed wasn't worth much.'

The street was not so crowded now. Maybe because the hour was late, or more likely on account of the wind that had begun to curl over the northern rim of the basin and push icy fingers through the town. The banners and outside lanterns swung and twisted above the heads of those night owls determined to sample all they could of High Mountain's pleasures before turning in. But there were no longer any strollers. Everyone hurried – to get in out of the strong wind or to reach where they were going before the place closed up.

Already, the church was darkened. One store was shuttered and another owner was in the process of closing, his head ducked against the weather as he took his wares in off the side-walk displays.

Edge had to look deep into the shadowed areas to see the handful of people who were not in any hurry to get someplace. For the all black attire of the Devil's Disciples made them difficult to pick out against the darkness of alleys and unlit door-ways.

'It's cold, Mr Edge,' Virginia said, and there was a note of complaint in her voice. 'You want to take a look at me instead of the damn street?' She lightened her tone. 'Before I hide my charms under the blanket?'

The half-breed shifted his gaze from the window to the whore and, under different circumstances, he might have felt a stirring of want. For the lines of her body had gained little from the dress she had now discarded. Her slender curves, just sensuously full enough at breasts and hips, were smooth and unblemished. Naked, she looked almost fragile, probably because of the stark whiteness of her flesh, relieved only at the crest of her firm breasts and the dense patch of hair triangled at the meeting of her thighs. Smiling, she did a slow pirouette for the benefit of his hooded, unblinking eyes. Her hair had been let down from the bun and it swung about her face – the features it brushed looking strangely innocent in the dim light filtering through the dusty window.

Not under any circumstances, would he have felt want for her. Because, despite all else he had become, his attitude towards whores had never altered. But as a whore, she was also a woman: and her nakedness and willingness would undoubtedly have caused a response in the pit of his stomach – if the need to stay alive had not been so pressing.

'You were right,' he muttered.

'About what?' She moved to the bed and slid under the covers.

Edge rechecked the view from the window. 'You got everything where it should be.'

'You don't sound overjoyed about that,' she muttered, complaining again.

The bodies of Joe and Harry and the carcase of the horse had been removed. But dark patches of dried blood on the street showed where they had fallen. Already, the wind was beginning to era e these signs.

Edge lowered his gear and rifle to the floor and moved to the dresser. He crouched in front of it and opened the doors beneath the drawer.

'You want to look under the damn bed, as well?' Virginia hissed.

Inside the dresser was a pitcher of water standing in a bowl. Edge lifted out the bowl, set it on the dresser top, filled it with water and dragged the dresser towards the window.

'What the hell?' the whore snarled, suddenly sitting upright.

Edge dug out his bankroll and peeled off two fives. He screwed them into a ball and tossed the money on to the bed. 'You owe me two bucks change, ma'am.'

She snatched at the money with a clawed hand and grinned. 'Maybe when we're through, you'll let me keep it for a tip.'

'Give you a tip before we start,' Edge responded, reaching up to the back of his neck and drawing the razor from its pouch. 'Give me no trouble and you'll still be able to wear low cut dresses.'

Virginia gasped as the razor's blade glinted in the low light. Then snatched at the blanket to hide her torso. 'Jesus, not one of them freaks!'

Edge had taken a tablet of soap from his gear. As he splashed water on to his face and lathered it, the whore gasped again. It was an expression of mixed surprise and relief.

'You ain't gonna screw me?'

'No, ma'am,' he answered, tilting the mirror to catch the available light. Then he began to rasp the bristles off his dark, deeply lined face.

'But you want more than a shave. You can get that at the barber's shop for just fifty cents.'

'You're not local?'

'Talk is all?'

'The kind that's worth seven dollars, ma'am. Figure a dollar for the use of the room and water. Doing my own shaving, so no service charge. Local whore wouldn't need to rent a room.'

'I'm from Denver. Came down when I heard about the music shindig. Was working out of a tent at the end of town before I heard this room was empty. Don't mind talkin' to a man. Makes a change.'

'How did Tallis get his bunch deputised?'

'That big local lawman didn't want it that way.'

'Ain't paying for information I already know,' Edge warned evenly.

'And I didn't hide my feelin's about them under a bushel? Always did talk too much.'

'Ever say anything worth listening too, ma'am?' There was a towel hanging from a peg on the side of the dresser and he used it to mop the surplus lather from his face.

'Okay,' she said with a broad grin, and lay down under the covers again. 'It makes a nice change to have a bed to myself.' She laughed and wriggled into a more comfortable position. 'I didn't get to High Mountain until after the Tallis creeps had it sewn up, but I soon got to hear what was happening. That bastard Sokalski told me I couldn't work here unless I paid Tallis a quarter of everythin' I earned.'

'Same for everybody in business here?' Edge asked, returning to the window after he had shoved the dresser back to its accustomed place.

'What do you think? Yeah, same for all the whores, all the storekeepers and like that. Even the local padre has to give twenty-five cents on every dollar for the artefacts he sells. Maybe the undertaker for burying, but I ain't sure about that.'

The polka dance finished in the meeting hall and the revellers scurried through the cold to their rented accommodation. Some to the temporary rooming houses along the street. Most to the tent town at the western end. Just a few entered the saloon, which, by the time Edge had finished shaving, was the sole source of noise in High Mountain. And even the sounds from below the whore's room were now subdued by weariness and the lateness of the hour. The music had ended and there was just talk, the clink of bottle necks against glass rims and the occasional burst of laughter. Plus the footfalls on the stairway and the opening and closing of doors.

'I ain't the only one who don't like it,' Virginia went on. 'But there ain't many of us. Seems the town councillors over-ruled High Fy to let in Tallis and his creeps. Had to, or this shindig would never have been held here. And it ain't only the whores that are making a big dollar from all these rich music lovers, Mr Edge. Reckon the sheriff's the only local citizen who ain't got an angle. And the take's big enough to cover the Tallis cut without hardship. Me and a couple of others just don't like the principle of it, that's all.'

'Big word, ma'am.'

She laughed again. 'Whores ain't just for screwin'. Lots of men talk a lot, too. A girl can learn if she's a mind.'

'Saw you were more than just a body,' the half-breed told her, still looking down the street. The banners and lamps swayed and turned above. Below, pieces of paper were rolled along the broad thoroughfare and swirled in the eddies created at alley mouths. The moan of the wind through narrow crevices was the loudest noise in town. 'Principle of having protection for a bunch of rich out-of-towners is fine.'

'Ain't no argument about that,' Virginia agreed. 'It's what sold the town councilmen into deputising them bastards. General opinion seems to be that they ain't the right kind, but they're all that's available.'

Directly across the street, the sheriff had moved from his desk to stand at the glass-panelled door of his office. He was

68

stooped, to peer expectantly out. Elsewhere, Edge saw four dark-clad figures standing in dark places, as unmoving as the buildings which cast shadows over them.

'Why d'you want to know about this?' the whore asked.

'My business,' the half-breed answered.

'Pardon me for askin'.'

'No sweat. Where's Tallis now?'

'He went up to Denver with Box – the guy who's running the shindig. Most of the other entertainment's already here. Come under their own steam. But this Rollo Stone group – seems they're big cheese. Gettin' the red carpet treatment. Heard talk they're real hard to please. Even the best's never good enough for them.'

'Just can't get no satisfaction, uh?' Edge said softly, and eased open the window.

'Hey, it's damn cold enough already!' Virginia snarled.

Edge ignored her as the familiar sounds of a rolling stage were borne into the room on the cold stream of air.

Across the street, the lawman had swung open his office door and stepped out onto the sidewalk. Edge eased the window wider and pushed his head through. As his face felt the icy touch of the mountain air, his slitted eyes raked the length of the street. He counted eleven black-garbed Devil's Disciples emerging from the shadows and then striding towards the hotel.

At the western end of the town, lamps were lit again, to supplement the light of fires and from the moon. Shouts were raised and people appeared. The Tallis men quickened their pace. The fast-moving stage rounded a bend in the trail where it cut through the tent town. Excited, half-dressed people scurried out of its path, then sprinted and stumbled in its wake as the driver worked to bring down the headlong pace of the team on High Mountain's street.

Lamplight began to shaft from the windows of the flanking buildings and doors were jerked open. Silhouetted forms clad in night clothes peered towards the source of the noisy excitement.

Below Edge's vantage point, the batswings were pushed open and held – by the two Devil's Disciples who had been killing time with cards and tooth picking. The gunmen from the shadows, studded lettering on their backs glinting in the overhead lamps, formed into two single files from the entrance a quarter of the way across the street.

'What's the ruckus?' the whore wanted to know, climbing from the bed and draping a blanket over her nakedness.

'Looking's still free in this town,' the half-breed replied, shifting so that she could see down into the street.

The big coach juddered to a halt outside the saloon and its nearside door swung open. Each Devil's Disciple raised a hand to fist a jutting gun butt. The excited crowd of out-of-towners, joined by a number of local citizens, broke from the strung-out throng behind the coach to swarm around it. The noise – of shouts, shrieks, cheers and hand-clapping – was louder than the earlier din of merry-making that had been spread through-out the town. For it was now concentrated in one small area – as the crowd pressed hard against the towering forms of the Devil's Disciples who had moved to close a defensive circle around the coach.

The black-garbed men snarled warnings at the excited sight-seers. But they were ignored – perhaps not heard above the tumult of other voices. And nobody looked into the gunmen's grim faces, for all eyes were directed at the coach.

'That's Tallis,' Virginia yelled, going up on her toes to put her lips close to his ear.

The leader of the Devil's Disciples had appeared at the open doorway of the coach, and the big vehicle tilted to one side as he put his weight on to the top step. Dressed in the same sombre style as his men, he was a good deal older, taller than most of them and bigger built than all. Close to fifty, he was grotesquely ugly, the lamplight shining on a face that emanated evil. The forehead was low, above deep-sunk dark eyes. The flesh of the cheeks hung in sacs, flanking a misshapen nose. His mouth was a long slash between bloodless lips, the jaw beneath pushed off centre by an old break that had not set back into its original line. The skin tone was the colour of unbaked dough, inscribed a dozen times on forehead, cheeks and jaw with the livid scars of ancient knife wounds. His head was square-shaped on a short neck between massive shoulders. Below, his torso seemed squat and disproportionate to his long, thick legs.

'The kind that stands out in a crowd,' Edge muttered as Ben Tallis thrust his muscular arms high into the air, then turned from the waist in both directions to survey the noisy crush of people.

'Six times meaner than he looks,' the whore shouted in the half-breed's ear. 'Got a whole lot more scars all over his body. Comanches did it and left him for dead.'

'Likely that changes a man's point of view,' Edge allowed as Tallis's unspoken demand for silence was obeyed.

'Hear tell he wasn't no Sunday-school teacher before the Injuns got to him,' Virginia said, and whispered now, for the moaning of the wind had become the only sound again.

'My friends!' Tallis roared, his voice as harsh to listen to as his face to look at. 'They are here and you will see them! But we must have restraint! My men are charged with the protection of all! You and those who will entertain you! '

As he spoke, displaying perfect teeth in what might have been a grin or a scowl, he continued to swing back and forth and raked his searching eyes over the eager faces of the watchers. The sheened back of his buckskin jacket was studded with the letters of his name.

'So keep your enthusiasm for the next three days, my friends!' he went on. 'And let us not have any unseemly incident to mar the arival of Mr Rollo Stone!'

As he spoke the name of the festival's main attraction, he leapt to the street. And another figure appeared in the doorway: tall, slim and youthful with a pale, angular face that expressed anxiety as roars and shrieks of greeting burst from more than two hundred throats. The young man snapped his head from side to side, then nodded at something Tallis yelled at him and shouted something of his own back into the coach before springing to the ground.

Three other youngsters stumbled over each other as they hurried out and rushed in the wake of Stone. The tumult of shouting rose in volume and the coach rocked as the crowd pressed closer. Then a barrage of abuse and warning was vented from the pulsing throats of the Devil's Disciples as they linked arms to hold back the crush.

The driver leapt down from his high seat and joined Tallis in helping to control the frenzied admirers of the musicians.

'Oh, no!' the whore gasped. 'Look!'

Edge didn't need her shaking hand to direct his attention towards the weak link in the human chain of gunmen. He had already spotted the fear in the face of one of the Devil's

Disciples. Then seen the man snatch his arm from around the waist of the black-garbed figure beside him and go for his gun.

Stone and his group were in a bunch, about to step up on to the sidewalk, when the protective ring was broken. The men to either side of the gap were pushed aside by the weight of the pressing crowd. Then, as the massive figure of Ben Tallis charged forward to close the opening, all but one woman held back.

She was a heavily built matron with her hair in curlers and a quilted robe wrapped around her bulky form. With an agile swerve and bob, she evaded the outstretched curve of Tallis's arm and lunged towards the quartet of musicians.

The group had halted momentarily on the sidewalk, to glance fearfully back as the break in the line was greeted by a renewed burst of frenzied sound.

In an instant, the noise was silenced – save only for a choked moan trailing from the matron's gaping mouth as she hurled herself towards Stone.

The blond youngster screamed, perhaps mistaking the woman's expression of hysterical adoration for a snarl of hatred. Fear rooted him where he stood and he could only thrust out his arms in a meek gesture of defence.

The gunmen who had panicked whirled free of the line, and drew his Colt.

'Don't, Nye!' Ben Tallis roared.

The crowd ceased to surge forward.

Sheriff Fyson leapt down from the opposite sidewalk and started to sprint across the street.

The matron clasped Stone's outstretched hands and fell hard to her knees. The three men around Stone clutched at his clothing as the woman tipped him towards her.

The Devil's Disciple squeezed the trigger of his Colt and its report silenced the start of a new vocal outburst. As a spray of crimson exploded from the back of the matron's head, she relinquished her grip on Stone's hands and prostrated herself at his feet. Stone screamed again – a strangled cry of horror – and was hauled upright by his colleagues.

The crowd backed away, those at the forefront again jostled by others at the back seeking a clearer view of death on the single street of High Mountain.

'Get inside!' Tallis roared at the quartet of musicians, then swung towards the killer as his order was obeyed. 'You crazy lunkhead!' he yelled, and drew his own gun.

'Hold it!' the sheriff snarled.

He had forced a way through the crowd and taken long strides around the rear of the stage. His Remington was out and as he came to a halt and issued the command, he swung the gun between Tallis and the man who had fired the shot.

'Real law business, goddamn it, Tallis!' He lowered his voice without taking any menace out of his words. 'I warned you, cousin. I warned you, goddamn it. No killing of innocent people!'

Rage made Tallis uglier than ever: twisting his mouthline, giving his dark eyes an evil glow and causing the slack, knife-scarred flesh of his cheeks to quiver. But he directed it for only part of a second towards Fyson. Then, pushing his half-drawn Colt back into the holster, he concentrated his powerful glower towards the shocked gunman. He did not utter a word or even lean closer to the luckless Devil's Disciple. But the man read a volume of meaning in the face and was transformed into a trembling wreck who bore no resemblance to his rigidly waiting partners.

'We'll discuss the matter, High Fy,' Tallis said at length, bringing his emotions under control and turning towards the sheriff. 'Seems like a mistake was made.'

'He can be real smooth when it suits him,' the whore whispered to Edge.

The half-breed ignored her as he rolled a cigarette from the makings taken from his shirt pocket.

'Get discussed in the meeting hall when circuit judge holds court there, cousin,' Fyson drawled. 'Week on Thursday.' He jerked the Remington towards the woman's killer. 'Drop the gun and move over to the law office, cousin.'

'Ben, you ain't gonna let me go to gaol?'

Tallis shifted his dark-eyed gaze towards his man, then looked beyond him as footfalls thudded hard against the saloon threshold.

'I'm backing you up against these varmints, Sheriff!' Hiram Rydell growled.

'Crazy kid,' Edge muttered as he lit the cigarette.

Tallis became the latest man to view Hiram's outlandish clothes with scorn. Then he sighed as he looked back towards Fyson. The sheriff had shown no reaction to Hiram's appearance from the saloon.

'It was a mistake, High Fy,' Tallis insisted softly. 'And we'll discuss it before a week on Thursday, I'm thinking. But you can take in my boy for now.'

There were sounds of disapproval from the ring of black-garbed figures, and a gasp of dismay from the man at the centre of the trouble. Tallis silenced the noise with an all-encompassing glare.

'Like I told the man!' he snapped. 'We'll talk it over about what Nye done. Law office has gotta be a better place than out here on the street with a norther set to blow!'

Another glare around the faces of the Devil's Disciples produced nods of agreement. And Nye even started to form a knowing grin as he dropped his gun. But the expression was driven off his features by the heavy menace emanated by Tallis's eyes. Then the ugly leader of the vigilantes thrust his hands high in the air again and swung back and forth to address the crowd.

'All right, friends,' he said grimly. 'It's been real tragic, but let's all learn from it. I asked you all to contain yourselves, didn't I? Be grateful now if you'd all return to your beds. Rest up and prepare yourself for the wonderful three days ahead of you. And let's hope the fine music you're gonna hear will help blot out of your minds what just happened here. Off you go, folks!'

He had yanked his hat brim low to shadow the burning emotion of his eyes. And his voice now had a soothing quality that was totally at odds with his previous demeanour.

The crowd responded to his plea, the people withdrawing from in front of the saloon to move with mournful slowness back to where they had come from. With the exception of Harvey Danby, who advanced to stoop beside the inert woman with the shattered skull.

'Dead as all get out,' the mortician reported to Fyson.

The sheriff sighed and nodded.

Tallis waved a hand as a sign of dispersal for his men, and all save Nye and another black-garbed figure moved away.

'That's Sokalski,' Virginia told Edge. 'Probably gonna tell his boss about you.'

'Let's us mosey on over to the cells,' Hiram growled, stepping down from the sidewalk and aiming both silver-plated guns at Nye.

'What in hell is that?' Tallis asked, interrupting the stream of whispered words Sokalski was pouring into his ear. He had pushed his hat on to the back of his head, to show that his eyes were brimming with more rage than ever. But his slash of a mouth was screwed into the line of a sneer as he pointed at Hiram.

'Young feller with a lot of guts, cousin,' the lawman answered.

'And no damn sense,' Edge muttered.

Tallis vented a harsh laugh. 'You're gonna need a lot more and a lot older if you figure to hold Nye, High Fy.'

'You and your varmints don't scare us none!' Hiram countered. He jabbed his guns into Nye's back. 'Move it, critter. Right on over to the slammer.'

Nye did so, but only after he had looked at Tallis and received a nod. Fyson scooped up the discarded murder gun before using his long strides to catch up with the prisoner and escort.

Tallis and his first lieutenant entered the saloon, the ugly man's face becoming totally captured by rage again as he heard Sokalski's report of the earlier shootings in High Mountain.

The stage driver began to off-load the roof baggage as the town mortician reappeared on the street, trundling a pushcart towards the sprawled corpse of the woman. After the law-office doorway had slammed closed, the squeak of the push-cart's wheels and the moan of the wind became the only competing sounds as lighted windows began to darken.

'No offence, but I'd rather not be close to you when Tallis evens the score,' Virginia muttered grimly.

Edge flicked his half-smoked cigarette out into the wind and lifted his rifle from against the wall. 'My trouble and nobody else's. Leave my stuff here?'

She shrugged, then grinned. 'For that two dollars I owe you?'

He nodded. 'But my loss is yours, if the gear goes missing? Who's that?'

As he closed the window, a short, rotund, round-faced man in a high hat, stiff collar and city suit emerged nervously from the stage.

The whore glanced down at him and broadened her grin. 'Guy who organised this whole festival shindig. He don't look it, but he's the best customer we whores got in this town – when he ain't in a high stakes poker game. Name's Duke Box.'

'Obliged for your help, ma'am,' the half-breed told her as he crossed to the door.

'You gonna stir up more trouble, Mr Edge?' Virginia asked anxiously. 'Because if you are, I reckon I'll hang around in the room for awhile.'

'Handle it if it happens,' he answered. 'But just aim to win me some money at poker is all. And if that feller likes high stakes, maybe I'll give Duke Box a play.'

Chapter Seven

THE saloon was still crowded beneath the cloud of blue tobacco smoke. But only with hard drinkers and heavy gamblers. Rollo Stone and the other three members of his ensemble had retired to their rooms after the long trip from Denver. And neither Ben Tallis nor any of his men were among those lined at the bar or seated at the tables.

But the trouble which would inevitably come to a violent head between the tall half-breed and the black-garbed gunmen was obviously on the mind of everyone who watched Edge descend the stairway. For, even though all returned immediately to low-voiced conversation or to cards after glancing briefly at him, Edge read the mixture of anxiety and excited anticipation in their eyes.

A way was cleared for him to the bar, and the sweating owner of the place hurriedly supplied him with a beer and a whiskey. Edge knew that, for once, it was not merely the latent menace which he always carried with him that caused the nervous shuffling nearby. Of greater concern to those who moved from him was the knowledge that one or more than a dozen guns might blast lead towards him at any moment.

'Obliged,' he told the man behind the bar as he offered payment and tipped the hard liquor into the foamed beer.

As he slowly sipped the drink, the noise level in the saloon returned to what it had been before he was spotted on the stairway. And the spaces on either side of him were filled. By a washed and shaved Augie on the right and the swaying, almost purple-faced British Baron on the left.

'I warned you, young feller,' the stage driver reminded with a rueful shake of his head. 'That Tallis and his bunch ain't the kind to tangle with. And all over gettin' a damn horse from one side of the street to the other.' He chewed on a wad of tobacco. 'Gotta be better reasons than that for dyin'.'

'The two men who attempted to stop him considered it worthwhile,' the Englishman countered. Although he had to lean heavily on the bar to keep from falling, his speech was no longer slurred. 'Not that it was merely the matter of the horse, I feel. There was the question of the pointing guns, was there not?'

'It bother you fellers?' Edge asked evenly, shifting his slitted eyes from one man to the other.

Augie shrugged. 'Like to see the whole damn Tallis bunch dead, mister. But that'll take more than just one man to do. Even a man like you.'

'I am merely interested in such a man as you, sir,' the Baron said. 'I am something of a student of human nature and I have never come across anybody like you before. Even when I served for Her Majesty's forces in India. I saw many who placed little value on human life – including their own. But all had a streak of madness in them. You, sir, are completely sane and as such there is a logical reason for everything you do. Which goes beyond such matters as weapons aimed at you and the need to move a horse from one point to another.'

'My business, feller,' Edge said, finishing the laced beer.

The Baron nodded. 'I realise that. And I do not question you, sir. But I trust you do not object to me studying you.'

'Great believer in education,' Edge allowed with a cold smile.

'My thanks,' the Baron replied, with a stiff bow that almost unbalanced him.

'No disrespect intended, young feller,' Augie said as Edge turned away from the bar. 'But I reckon it'll be the Tallis bunch that'll be teachin' lessons.'

The half-breed broadened the smile that did not extend beyond the deep lines cutting away from the corners of his thin lips. 'You're entitled to your school of thought, feller.'

He moved casually among the tables, towards a corner of the room where the poker game with the largest stakes was taking place. Six shirt-sleeved men were already seated around the money-littered table and the dapper-dressed Duke Box was standing nearby – first in line to fill a vacant chair. But two players were showing signs of retirement from the game. One was having trouble keeping his eyes open and a second mopped frantically at his brow every time he glanced down at the meagre remains of his depleted stake.

Edge leaned his back against the wall, rifle still canted to his shoulder, and carefully watched the players and the play.

He was out ten thousand dollars after his run-in with Sullivan and the Apache renegades and, second in line of his priorities – after staying alive – was to replace what had been lost. He had only to watch three hands of the five card stud to know he had a good chance of achieving his aim in coming to High Mountain. For the players were rich enough to provide the bankroll and, after Box had replaced the exhausted man, only two of them were experts on the subtleties of the wild card game. Which, in a six-chair school, meant that three were ripe to be taken.

The only factor working against the half-breed's plan was time and Ben Tallis was in control of that. But, from what the whore had told him and based on the evidence of his own eyes, Edge was sure he would receive advance warning of the trouble to come. Provided he stayed away from dark and deserted places where the Devil's Disciples merged into the shadows.

'You wiped me out, gentlemen,' the player who had sweated a lot announced when another pot was taken. 'I'm for bed and regrets.'

'Any objections?' Edge asked, gripping the back of the chair with a brown-skinned hand as it was vacated.

'If you know the rules and have the money, none,' Box answered, his round fifty-year-old face wreathed with a beam as he gathered up the cards for his deal.

The other four men at the table expressed their discontent without speaking. Until one whispered: 'He's the feller that shot two of Ben's boys, Duke.'

Box bobbed his head. 'Figured that out for myself, gents. When he showed up on the stairs it was like most gents in this place saw a ghost.' He brightened the smile and waved for

Edge to take the chair. 'But he ain't so dumb as that shoot-out makes him look. Knows same as me – and same as you gents oughta – that Ben Tallis ain't gonna do nothin' about him until Ben Tallis is good and ready to pick where, when and how.'

Edge sat down and nodded in acknowledgement as he leaned the Winchester against the chair. 'Man has to be careful about rocking this kind of showboat – especially when he's getting twenty-five per cent of what the passengers pay for being taken for a ride?'

'This game's private,' the little entrepreneur said, dealing the cards around the table. 'No house share. Five card stud. Dealer calls wild or not. No stake limit and no markers. Hard cash only.'

Edge put his money on the table in front of him. A few dollars more than two hundred and seventy – the money he had been paid for his dead horse, the reward on the two hold-up men he had killed and what was left of the pay he had earned at Fort Hope.

He had played five games, and almost doubled his bankroll by taking one pot, when the bellowing voice of Ben Tallis sounded out on the street.

'Duke! Me and the boys are pullin' outta this town!'

The half-breed was in the process of dealing as the harsh-spoken words cut across the moan of the strengthening norther. He reacted with just a further narrowing of his hooded eyes in the shadow of his hat brim – and continued with the deal. But Box ended the game by leaping to his feet and snatching his hat from the floor beside his chair.

'What the hell!' he snapped, jamming the hat on his head as he stormed towards the door, swinging his short arms to force a way through the other saloon patrons who were crowding in the same direction.

'Has to be another way down and out from upstairs,' Edge said evenly as the other players showed indecision about whether to remain at the table or move to see the outcome of the new disturbance in High Mountain.

'Outside stairway at the rear,' one of the men supplied.

'Obliged,' Edge said, picking up his money and his rifle and pushing back his chair. 'Finish the game another time?'

He raked his glinting eyes around their faces and each responded with a reluctant nod.

'Hey, Ben!' Box yelled as he reached the sidewalk. 'What you and the boys doin' for Christsake?'

'I told you, Duke! Pullin' out! Can't do our job of protectin' people if my boys get arrested for doin' it!'

Only Augie and the Baron were still at the bar, their liquor-glazed eyes following Edge as the half-breed took the stairs two at a time.

'That Tallis is smart,' the stage driver growled as Edge was lost in the smoke haze. 'He ain't gonna pull out.'

'Seems our fellow-traveller is equally aware of that fact, sir,' the Englishman said. 'I'll be gravely disappointed if he keeps on running.'

'He'll be in a grave if he don't,' Augie countered.

As he moved along the balcony, Edge could still hear the exchange out on the wind-blown street.

'I'll talk to the sheriff!' Box yelled. 'He can't handle this alone!'

Edge pushed open the door of Virginia's room, moved silently inside, and closed it after him. The whore was still enjoying her lone rest, sprawled out on her stomach under the blanket cover. She did not move as the half-breed crossed the room and eased open the window a crack.

'High and mighty Sheriff Fyson ain't in no mood to listen to nobody, Duke!' Tallis snarled.

The sounds of the weather had been loud enough to mask the movement of horses. More than twenty of them, reined into a close-knit, unmoving group between the saloon and the law office. Each mount was straddled by a black-garbed gunman with studded lettering on his back. Big, strong-looking stallions, finely curried and tacked out with polished black leather saddles and bridles glinting with metalwork trim.

'We'll damn well see about that!' Box yelled, and stepped down off the sidewalk to cross the street.

The door of the law office swung open as the rotund form of Box drew level with where the ugly Ben Tallis sat on his horse. And the lawman ducked his head under the lintel to step outside. The tall Hiram Rydell looked almost slight beside the towering figure of Fyson.

'Law has to take its proper course, cousin!' Fyson drawled. 'Ain't turning loose a man that shot an unarmed female in the back.'

The loud exchange of voices disturbed the sleeping citizens of High Mountain yet again. Light spilled from windows and

6   81

doors jerked open. The word spread fast along the length of the single street. And reached the tent town.

'Sheriff!' Box snarled. 'The man was a duly deputised law officer who made a genuine mistake! Do you realise what will happen if Ben Tallis pulls out with his men?' He flung out both arms to point each way along the street. 'We got some of the wealthiest folks in the West here in High Mountain. And they already spent a small fortune with the businessmen hereabouts.'

Edge saw the knowing grin on the knife-scarred face of Tallis as the leader of the vigilantes turned to look towards the crowd moving along the street from the tent town.

'The bad element has only been kept out because they know we have fine protection. Do you think they will stay out when they hear all we have is a sheriff?'

'Dang it, two notches on my shooting iron means I ain't no tenderfoot no more!' Hiram yelled, and hitched up his gunbelt.

The advance of the out-of-towners had halted short of the group of horsemen. A half-dozen were listening intently as the bald-headed horse trader explained what the new arrivals had missed of the exchange. The town's mortician and the owner of the Peaks Saloon and Hotel hurried across to join the discussion.

Hiram was again ignored.

'Town'll be wide open for any trigger happy thief to walk in and take what he wants!' Box continued. 'But there won't be just one. Every crook west of the Mississippi will head for High Mountain.' His tone became scornful. 'You're big and you're broad, High Fy. But ain't no one man big enough to handle the hell that'll break loose if Ben and his boys move out.'

'Dang me, I already – ' Hiram started, his youthful face inscribed with rising anger.

'Keep it shut, boy!' the lawman told him. 'Real talk's just about to start.'

Danby and one of the out-of-towners had broken from the front of the crowd, to circle around the horsemen and join Box. Fyson watched them with wary eyes, and his tight mouth was drawn into a thinner line.

'I don't like this, High Fy,' the skinny mortician announced. 'But it's gotta be done. I'm speaking for the town councilmen – and most of the people of High Mountain, I reckon. This here feller reckons he can get the backin' of all the folks that come to the festival.'

The man at his side was short and broadly built with white hair and a pale face. He had to clear his throat before he could make his voice heard above the wind from the north.

'No disrespect intended, Sheriff. But we strangers to this town have no confidence in the ability of you and that young boy to protect our persons and property. Should Mr Tallis and his men leave, then so shall we. I have not canvassed all those involved, but I feel I can – '

'And I ain't spoken to all our folks,' Danby cut in. 'But I'm damn sure none of them want to lose the kinda business been brought here by the festival. You want a vote taken, I'll fix it. But you know which way it'll go. And you know the town councilmen got the right to suspend you from office – on the grounds of dereliction of duty. Reckon we got them grounds in this case.'

Stretched seconds of silence followed the mortician's final word – broken only by the moan of the wind and the flapping of the overhead canvas signs. The lawman's expression had not altered as he listened to the threat. And it remained hard as he raised his right hand to the left side of his chest and lifted the tin star off his shirt pocket. He weighed the badge in the palm of his big hand for a moment, then flipped it out into the street. It was heavy enough to maintain an intended course through the wind, and hit the ground between Danby's boots.

'When a man resigns, Harv, no need for a vote to be taken. Wouldn't want any one to lose business on account of me. But I reckon you could become the busiest man in town, cousin.'

He unhooked the ring of keys from his belt and said something to Hiram as he handed it to the youngster. The kid was as surprised as most other people at the ease with which Fyson had surrendered his office: and he turned like a robot to go back inside and through into the cell block. Then this initial reaction was replaced by relief on many of the cold-pinched faces: and only those who happened to see the brief grin of triumph flit across the grotesquely ugly face of Ben Tallis experienced a tremor of foreboding that the black-garbed man and his followers were now entirely in control of law and order in High Mountain.

Fyson's long legs carried him across to the saloon in a short time without any show of haste. Danby and the spokesman

83

for the out-of-towners moved back from whence they came with far less dignity. The released prisoner swaggered from the law office, hand raised in response to the cheers and ribald congratulations of his partners. The dudish attire of Hiram Rydell looked even more inappropriate as the kid reappeared, head hung low and shoulders stooped in an attitude of dejection.

As Tallis and Box became engaged in a low-voiced conversation, the crowd of bystanders broke up – to return to the saloon or to their beds.

Edge remained at the cracked-open window, feeling a tight ball of anger at the pit of his stomach. He was still better than nine grand short of the reason he had come to High Mountain and he had no chance of making up the difference while Tallis ran the town. But no part of the coldly controlled rage was directed at himself, for none was aroused by the irrefutable fact that he had created the difficulty by his own actions.

The drunken Englishman had been wrong in his opinion that the half-breed only acted for a logical purpose – if the Baron had judged Edge by the standards of normal men. But perhaps his perception was still as strong as it had been at the scene of the hold-up, despite all the liquor he had poured into himself since then. Maybe he recognised that the man called Edge had more in common – emotionally – with a cougar than with his fellow human beings. And that for him to act instinctively was not a sign of irrationality, merely a valid aspect of the character which cruel fate had forced him to adopt.

Two men had tried to prevent him from doing what he wanted to do. He had warned them – always he warned those who blocked his way, if there was time. They had ignored the warning and so they had died. Such an occurrence in the harsh life of the half-breed was an inevitable result of the circumstances which created it – and at the moment of its staging was completely divorced from its ramifications. Much as a cougar must hunt and kill its prey to live, even while those who seek to kill it may be closing in.

To back down from the menace of aimed guns did not kill a man but, to a man like Edge it would take away something of what he had become. And what he had become was all he had.

'I sure hope it ain't me you're mad at,' Virginia rasped from the bed.

She had been watching him for a full minute, having been roused from sleep by a sense of another's presence in the room. And while she watched, she had seen the tautness of his anger set his profile into even harder lines than usual. Now, as he shifted his gaze towards her, she caught a glimpse of the blue fires in his slitted eyes when they reflected the light from outside.

'Go get that murderin' bastard!' Tallis roared from the street below. 'You hear that, Edge? You're gonna be got, man and you're gonna be got good! Nobody messes with the Devil's Disciples and gets away with it!'

'Set your mind at rest, ma'am?' the half-breed asked softly as he shifted his gaze back to the street.

It was empty of all except the black-garbed men. Tallis stood on the sidewalk in front of the law office, moving his head from side to side to direct his threat towards both ends of town. One hand was draped over his jutting Colt butt while the other fixed Fyson's discarded badge to the front of his jacket. Four of his men were leading away the horses. The remainder stood in a rock solid group at the centre of the street, rigid against the buffetting of the wind.

'Not if they find you here with me,' the whore answered nervously.

A curt nod from Tallis was the signal for his men to break from the group and fan out to cover the town. Two of them moved on the entrance of the saloon. Another went into the alley that gave on to the rear of the place.

'Leave my gear here still?' Edge asked as he rose from digging a carton of .44 shells from the saddlebag.

'Talk about extra charge if you're still alive to pay it,' she allowed as he moved to the door. 'Hey, how come High Fy's lettin' Tallis get away with this?'

Edge cracked open the door and peered outside. 'Guess you could say he's resigned to the situation,' he muttered, and stepped out on to the balcony.

Chapter Eight

'HE was in here!' Sokalski yelled across the saloon.

'Right,' Box responded. 'Was playin' cards with us. Didn't see him leave.'

'Any of you others?' Sokalski's partner demanded. 'We're all the law this town's got now and you'd better not hinder us.'

'Everyone was watching the events outside, my good man,' the Baron lied, and caused Edge's lips to curl back in a cold smile as the half-breed strode silently around the balcony.

A glance over the rail showed that the patrons of the saloon had resumed what they had been doing before Tallis had started his tactical ploy to gain control of High Mountain's law. Through the slowly moving layer of blue smoke, he saw that the three poker games were underway again and that the heavy drinkers were lined up at the bar.

Hiram was at the counter, standing between Augie and the Baron. He was drinking whiskey from a beer glass, shuddering as each gulp burned its way down his throat.

The ex-sheriff sat alone at a table, sipping beer with apparent relish and seeming to ignore what was happening around him.

The two Devil's Disciples were flanking the entrance, right hands fisted around gun butts. But the Colts remained in the low-slung holsters as the men scoured the malodorous, now silent room with demanding eyes.

The owner of the place mopped at his sheened brow with his apron as the hard stares of the black-garbed men fixed upon his face. Then he issued a tacit reply to the unspoken question – he rolled his eyes up in their sockets to indicate the first floor of the building.

Another of their number died as the two gunmen lunged away from the batswings to sprint for the foot of the stairs.

Edge had moved half way around the balcony and entered a short passage between two room doors. Light which spilled up on to the balcony from the lamps in the saloon did not penetrate into the passage and the half-breed was in pitch darkness when he reached the door at the end. Draughts of cold air from cracks between the door and frame told him that he was only a pace away from the dangerous freedom of the moonlit night. Footfalls thudding on the stairs warned him of the kind of danger that was out there.

He felt for the hinges and discovered the door opened inwards. The man running up the steps rose closer. Edge lay his rifle on the floor at the base of the wall, drew the razor with his right hand and curled the fingers of his left around the doorknob. Then he went down into a half crouch and tensed his muscles.

The man outside reached the top of the stairs, broke stride, and fisted a hand around the knob. Edge allowed him to turn it, then closed his grip and yanked at the door.

Below in the saloon, the two Devil's Disciples thudded their feet against the floor boarding. The sound covered the small yelp of surprise from the man on the outside stairway.

'Edge!' Hiram yelled in warning as the two gunmen started up the inner stairs.

The man outside was jerked across the threshold – for an instant his left hand was as tight around the doorknob as his right was fisted on the butt of his drawn Colt.

'No introductions necessary, kid,' the half-breed muttered as his right arm swung towards the shocked face of the Devil's Disciple.

As he spoke the final word, his victim released his hold on the doorknob. But the man had no time to get off a shot from the Colt. He was folded forward from the waist, his head held up to stare at the half-crouched form of Edge silhouetted against the saloon lights. This attitude exposed the full length of his neck, from the point of the jaw to the top of his kerchief.

The sharpened point of the blade sank deep into the skin just below the Adam's apple. It drove deep to slice through the jugular vein and puncture the windpipe. The man's gasp ended with a moist gurgle and he fell to his knees as he dropped the Colt. He lived for a moment more, to stare regretfully up into the impassive face of his killer. Then he tilted to the side and toppled, his own weight drawing him off the deadly blade. His death rattle powered a great gush of blood from the wound as the unorthodox weapon came clear of the flesh.

'Hey, Yale!' Sokalski yelled as he raced up the stairs and Edge snatched up the Winchester. 'The bastard's in here, Yale!'

The half-breed's lips curled back and his eyes narrowed to glinting slits as he stepped over the corpse slumped on the threshold. 'Seems your buddies are going to reach deadlock,' he rasped.

Bright moonlight bathed the back lots of the buildings lining the southern side of the street, but patterned it with contrasting patches of deep shadow. Beyond, the rising ground of the basin offered little cover except the growing crops of wheat and sugar beet.

The wind rippled the plantings like the waves of a dry sea. Closer, it lifted and swirled the litter of town living around the corners of the buildings. But nothing more substantial than this was moving until Edge, ignoring the stairway, leapt down from the outside landing. He hit the ground sure-footed, legs bent and braced to absorb the impact, then powered forward as part of the same fluid movement.

For part of a second, he saw a man in silhouette through a rear window of the saloon, peering out across the back lot. A man so tall that he had to go down into a deep stoop to see beneath the lintel.

Then Edge ducked into the rear porch of the meeting hall, pumping the action of the Winchester as he withdrew into the shadows. Behind him, the wind obliterated his footprints in the dust an instant after he had made them. And a moment after he gained cover, three horsemen galloped their mounts from around the side of the stage line office, one of them leading a riderless animal. All four raised a cloud of dust as they skidded to a halt at the foot of the stairway. The moaning norther snatched at the billowing particles and hurled them out across the fields.

The trio of riders were encased in ankle-length coats and their horses were a mixture of greys and chestnuts, geldings and mares. The narrowed eyes of the half-breed recognised a chestnut gelding as one of the horses that had been brought to High Mountain behind the Concord coach. Then, as the men looked up towards the head of the stairs, he recognised two faces – the tooth picker and solitaire player who had been in the saloon when he first entered.

Another man appeared on the landing and peered down. 'Grummond?'

'Who friggin' else?'

'The bastard's killed Yale! Slit his friggin' throat, frig it!'

All four snapped their heads from side to side, worried eyes raking over the shadowed buildings. Edge pressed his back against the meeting-hall door and loosened his double-handed grip of the Winchester held slantwise across his chest. But the searching eyes failed to spot him.

'So Yale makes it look even better,' Grummond called up. 'You got him?'

'What you want him for?' the man replied, surprised.

'Stone, dummy!' Grummond snarled.

'Sokalski's handlin' it. I better cover him!'

He stepped back inside, over the corpse of Yale, while Grummond remained in the saddle – a hand resting on his booted rifle and his eyes resuming the careful search of the buildings – and the other two men dismounted. One of these started up the stairway as the other lifted the lariat from his own horse and moved to the spare mount.

Edge remained unmoving in the shadows, his lean features set in impassive lines that betrayed nothing of what he was thinking.

There was shouting inside the Peaks Saloon and Hotel and out on the street beyond. But the sounds created by the wind blurred the words.

Sokalski stepped out on to the landing, a nightshirt-clad form draped across his arms. He came down the stairway and transferred his burden to the other man.

'I don't like it we ain't got that bastard Edge, Sol,' the man complained. 'He could be watchin' us right now.'

'He's long gone, or Ben'll handle him,' Sokalski snarled.

'You guys just get this jerk up to the Hole and do like you're supposed to!'

He swung around, raced to the top of the steps and stooped to pick up Yale before disappearing inside the building. The slumped, unconscious form of Rollo Stone was carried to the ground and, while Grummond cursed at the others to hurry, it was lashed to the saddle of the spare mount. Then the two men swung astride their horses. The animals wheeled, then were heeled into a gallop – due south from the rear of the building, pumping hooves trampling the crops until the kidnappers veered to the side and raced up the trail towards the distant pass.

Edge watched them for a few moments, then tried the door of the meeting hall. It was unlocked and swung open under gentle pressure. Inside, the cold air still smelled of cigar smoke, liquor and perfume from the polka dance. Moonlight through the windows showed an empty central space with chairs and tables enclosing it. The half-breed's long legs carried him fast to one of the windows flanking the double front doors of the hall's main entrance. He lifted the window just a fraction, to admit a biting stream of colder air – and the sounds of the latest disturbance to hit High Mountain this troubled night.

He reached his vantage point in time to see Ben Tallis lunge from the doorway of the law office in response to a shout from Sokalski.

'The bastard's got Stone, Ben! Him and some others! They killed Yale!'

As the massive figure of Tallis came to a halt in the centre of the street, the rear door of the meeting hall swung open. Edge tightened his grip on the Winchester, but turned just his head to look over his shoulder. Another big man stepped out on to the moonlit former dance-floor .

'Only me, cousin,' Fyson drawled.

'Figured it might be,' Edge answered, and resumed his watch on the street.

'Saw you and what happened. Through the window. Got out the same window. Nobody saw me. Except you, I guess.'

He advanced nonchalantly towards the half-breed, his big hands thrust deep into his hip pockets.

'For a man that came looking for a big game, you sure got into a rough one, cousin,' the former sheriff continued blandly.

'Tallis started this deal long before I showed up, feller,' Edge answered. 'Seems I'm just a side bet he plans to take along with the pot.'

'Yeah, cousin,' Fyson agreed as he towered over the tall Edge for a moment, then stooped to peer out of the window. 'I been waiting for something like this to happen, ever since that bunch got here. Ben Tallis being what he is.'

'What is he?' the half-breed asked as the ugly leader of the vigilantes was joined at the centre of the street by Sokalski. 'Apart from an ugly bastard – and I ain't one to hold the way a man looks against him.

'One-time buffalo hunter until the Comanches carved him up for killing a squaw. Then a peace officer up in some town in Northern California. Got his badge taken away for hanging a man before the trial.'

Tallis and Sokalski were engaged in deep conversation, most of it about a sheet of paper the latter had brought out of the saloon.

'Had six deputies that got fired along with him. Went on a hell-raising spree from one end of the state to the other. Didn't commit no bad crimes. Just raised Cain – and the small army you seen here in High Mountain.'

'I figure this joker's part of it, Ben!' the other Devil's Disciple who had been in the saloon yelled. 'Shouted a warnin' that we was comin' after Edge.'

Hiram Rydell stumbled into the field of vision from the window. The black-garbed man moved up behind him, still aiming the two silver-plated Colts he had used to shove the youngster forward.

'Started to hire himself and his men out,' Fyson went on in the same flat tone of voice as Edge gave a low grunt of irritation. 'Guards, escorts, private policing jobs. High charges and something always went wrong. But worked so no blame falls on Tallis and his bunch. And always some killings or bad beatings to keep down the rumours.'

'I ain't no two-bit kidnapper!' Hiram snarled as he pulled up short in front of Tallis and Sokalski.

'I know you're not, punk!' Tallis yelled, and once more swung his head from side to side to direct his harsh voice along the length of the street. He held the piece of paper high and waved it violently, clutching it tight against the tug of the wind. 'This here ransom note prices you higher than that!'

Tallis was playing to an audience again, but this time he did not allow even a momentary grin to alter the lines of the grim expression etched into the tortured flesh of his face.

'Fifty thousand dollars!' he roared towards the crowd approaching from one end of the street, then swung to look in the opposite direction – from where more shocked, weary-eyed people were advancing. 'Fifty thousand dollars! That's what this guy Edge and his helpers are demanding for the return of Rollo Stone!' He glowered at Hiram and the young dude's veneer of toughness showed cracks under the strain of holding the vicious gaze.

Then the kid finally managed to tear his eyes away from the trap of the enraged glower and he wrenched his head from side to side and stared back over his shoulder. The advancing crowds were swelling in size by the moment, as more people emerged from the buildings. Lamplight shafting from almost every window and doorway in town turned night into day: bright enough so that nobody noticed when storm clouds raced across the sky to blot out the moon.

'Has to make it look like he's on the side of the law,' the ex-sheriff drawled. 'So he can get another job for his bunch. Takes more organisation, but it beats being your hit-and-run type outlaw, uh cousin? Tallis is a real smart feller.'

'One might say positively devilish, sir,' Baron Finn-Jenkins called softly.

Both Edge and Fyson started to turn, the half-breed swinging the rifle and the taller man going for his Remington. Then they recognised the familiar cultured tones of the Englishman, froze, and relaxed as they returned their attention to the street.

'It's proof of what I claimed!' Tallis bellowed to his audience of townspeople and visitors, with a sprinkling of his own men spread amongst them. 'The kidnappers struck while my protection was lifted from High Mountain! Let it be a lesson to you people! But don't you fret about young Stone, you hear! Me and my men are back in business! And the man you all came to see will be back here to play for you tomorrow! You have the word of Ben Tallis on that!'

He brought both hands down to his sides, then nodded towards the law office and rasped an order at Sokalski and another at the man behind Hiram. Sokalski spun to head back towards the saloon while Hiram was forced across to the law office, his own fancy guns held hard against the small of his back.

'All you folks return to your beds!' Tallis yelled. 'You won't be disturbed no more tonight!'

Then he turned to stride in the wake of Hiram and the kid's captor. For a few moments, the watchers remained where they were. Then the first spots of icy rain were flung down at them, and this did more than the urgings of the Devil's Disciples to send the crowds of people scurrying back towards warmth and shelter.

This first flurry of wetness turned abruptly to a downpour of sleet, falling as hard and thick as during the storm among the high peaks.

But before the weather drew a constantly moving curtain along the street, the watchers at the meeting hall window saw the first three moves which opened the next phase of Tallis's plan. Firstly, as the Englishman crouched down between Edge and Fyson, the Devil's Disciples who had been left in stark isolation on the street as the crowds broke up once more fanned out to recommence their search of the town's buildings. Then, in the law office, Hiram Rydell swung round to face Ben Tallis. The man behind the kid shoved him hard in the back and Hiram was flung forward. Hiram's mouth gaped in fear, then was crunched closed as Tallis's fist smashed into his jaw. The young dude staggered backwards, and collapsed into the open arms of the man behind him. He was hauled towards the door giving on to the cell block. Blood trickled down from both corners of his mouth. Finally, Sokalski emerged from the saloon, followed by the dapper-dressed Duke Box, and both ducked their heads against the wind-driven sleet as they hurried across the street.

'You don't look like the kind that moves the way a hunting Apache does, feller,' Edge muttered as he shifted his gaze to the Baron. His hooded eyes still glinted more brightly than usual – with the fires of a cold anger that had erupted at the sight of Hiram Rydell going down under the brutal attack.

As the three men drew themselves erect at the window, the rigid stance of the Englishman and the man's grim expression gave no hint that he had been close to falling down drunk a few minutes ago.

'And you do not look the kind to allow his judgement to be clouded by a foolish young boy, sir,' the Baron replied distinctly. 'Just as, until now, Sheriff Fyson showed no sign of being a man of action. But appearances can be deceptive, can they not?'

'I was damn sure nobody saw me, goddamn it!'

'Only I, sir,' the Baron assured. 'And I was late in joining you because I needed to be certain nobody saw me. All attention was diverted to the street.'

'What's your interest, cousin?' Fyson demanded.

'I would suggest we find a more secure place than this to discuss matters of mutual interest, gentlemen. Those thugs in black are not wandering about in this foul weather because they enjoy it.'

'He talks funny, but he talks sense,' Fyson drawled with a meaningful look at Edge. 'Tallis won't have this wrapped up tight until you're dead, cousin.'

'Quite so,' the Englishman agreed. 'I think the first thing to do is leave town for a place where we may plan our campaign.'

'Wrong, cousin,' Fyson countered. 'First thing we do is get us a Tallis man and find out where they took Stone.'

'Place called the Hole,' Edge supplied.

Fyson grinned. 'Livermore Hole?'

'Just said the Hole, feller.'

The Englishman smiled now. 'Very well. We can make our way there, recover the unfortunate Mr Stone and then plan our next move.'

His glance towards the half-breed invited agreement.

'Seems there ain't a lot of mutual interest, feller,' Edge replied, moving from the window to the front door of the meeting hall. 'Aim to spring Hiram out of gaol before I do anything else.'

The Baron sighed. 'Not a very auspicious start to our alliance,' he complained.

'Ain't that what a musical event like an open-air festival is all about?' Edge said as he pulled open one of the two doors.

'How's that, cousin?' the towering Fyson drawled.

The half-breed glanced over his shoulder as he stepped out into the storm. 'Everyone doing his own thing.'

Chapter Nine

THE few lighted windows and the many lanterns that were strung overhead were disembodied patches of blurred brightness through the wind-driven sleet. Edge and the two men who followed him out of the meeting hall were like wraiths as they moved to the centre of the street.

Neither Fyson nor Baron Finn-Jenkins had anything to fear from the prowling Devil's Disciples – unless they were seen with the half-breed. But the centre of the broad thoroughfare was probably the safest place in town to hold a hurried discussion – for as long as the minor blizzard continued to billow its wet curtain of falling sleet around the trio. Because the men searching nervously for Edge were concentrating their attention on the more obvious hiding places among the flanking buildings.

It was the Englishman who did most of the talking, his lips moving fast beneath the bushy moustache turned white by clinging sleet. When he was finished, the half-breed vented a grunt of acknowledgement.

'Sounds all right, cousin,' Fyson said.

Then they split up and in a moment were lost to each other's sight. Fyson took long, easy strides towards the front of the law office. The Baron, dropping back into his pose as a drunk, weaved along the centre of the street, before veering in the direction of the livery. Edge went into the alley between the law office and the church, cocked rifle canted to his shoulder and right hand scratching the side of his jaw – six inches from the handle of the razor nestled against the nape of his neck.

He heard the door of the office open, then the even drawl of Fyson's voice.

'Evening, cousins. Just come over to see if I can help any On account of – '

The door closed to curtail the ex-lawman's offer and to mask whatever responses greeted it.

Edge moved silently and quickly down the length of the alley, empty now of the Concord and horses. He stayed close to the stone wall of the office, then the cell block, narrowed eyes peering through the storm-lashed darkness and ears strained to catch the slightest sound not caused by the blizzard.

Menace lurked just beyond the curtaining downpour but came no closer. At the rear of the building, the half-breed put his cold and tension-stiffened face close to one of the two barred apertures. Just enough light from the office filtered through the cracks around the closed door to show shadowy shapes inside the cell block. And he moved to the other glass-less window, to look down on Hiram Rydell – still crumpled on the floor of the cell where he had been dumped.

The voices of Fyson, Tallis, Sokalski and Box were an indistinct mumbling from the far side of the door. The kid's ragged breathing was louder. Then he grunted and gasped as Edge dropped a handful of scooped up mud on to his face. He jerked his legs and flailed his arms.

'Just want you awake, Hiram,' the half-breed rasped. 'Not the whole damn town.'

The kid shook his head. 'Who is it?' he croaked.

'Didn't your folks warn you to stay away from bars?' Edge countered wryly, pressing his face closer to the grille.

The young dude sat up and snapped his head from side to side, recalling where he was and why he was there. He heard the mumble of voices, saw the familiar lean face at the window, and used the side of the cot to haul himself upright. Edge showed a fleeting grin as Hiram snatched up the ten gallon hat and jammed it on his head.

'You gonna get me outta this calaboose, doggone it?' the kid asked, moving close to the window. There was no anxiety in his voice and the blood and mud streaked across his face added a quality of surface toughness to his youthful features.

'Figure to parole you, Hiram,' Edge muttered.

'Beat a rug, you sure changed your tune from awhile back. Didn't want a tenderfoot like me near you.'

'Ain't nothing changed about that.'

'What's the plan?'

'Listen and hear,' the half-breed growled. 'When you break loose, some hell's going to do the same thing.' He jerked a thumb over his shoulder. 'And you run like that hell.' He showed another brief smile. 'Thataway. Then you circle the town and go into the hotel by the back stairs. You look for room number five. You check that the whore inside ain't got a customer and then you go in. Her name's Virginia. You tell her I said you're staying with her. Same arrangement as for my gear.'

'Aw, shoot!' the kid complained. 'I'll be a sitting duck for them Devil's Disciples critters!'

Edge shook his head. 'No arguments, Hiram. Tallis will figure you're with me and I won't be in town.'

'What if I won't do it, dang it?'

'No sweat, Hiram,' Edge told him grimly. 'Soon as you're out of here, we're even.'

'Even for what?' He was puzzled.

'The hold-up, feller. Hadn't been for you, we'd all be dead. Most important, I'd be dead.'

'That works both ways, Edge.'

Edge spat to the side. 'You want to talk yourself out of being busted out, Hiram?'

'No, sir, I sure enough don't.'

'So stay quiet and wait.'

'For what?'

'Help.'

'I'm getting the impression you're a man who doesn't welcome favours,' the young dude said, his expression pensive and his speech reverting to the accents of his proper environment.

'You being out of here is only part of what I want, Hiram,' Edge rasped. 'And they need me as much as I need them for the rest of it.'

'Which was how it was at the hold-up?' Hiram grinned, and the humour robbed his dark-streaked face of the impression of toughness.

The anger which tautened the lines of the half-breed's lean features was evenly divided this time – directed towards Hiram Rydell and inwards. Then the expression became impassive and he held up a warning hand to silence another comment forming on the kid's lips.

Footfalls sounded, from the direction of the rear of the church – and the livery stables were in the opposite direction.

'If that mean-lookin' drifter's got any sense, he'll be long gone from here by now,' a man growled.

Another man spat as the footfalls halted. 'If he ran, he won't last long on foot without shelter in this. I can feel myself freezin' up in my joints.'

Edge leaned closer to the bars and whispered softly to the kid, who grinned, nodded vigorously and accepted the two weapons that were handed to him.

'He sure won't be hangin' around this place, that's for damn sure,' one of the pair of Devil's Disciples said as they started forward again, crossing the alley at an angle to go around the rear of the cell block.

Edge flattened himself to the stone wall, Winchester levelled across his belly and aimed at the point where the men would appear. Then, as the two forms swung around the corner, he folded away from the wall and tracked the rifle barrel between the bellies of the men. They came to a halt with gasps of shock, and instinctively reached for their holstered revolvers.

'Don't plan to shoot you!' Edge said conversationally.

The men's arms halted, hands hovering close to the jutting butts of their Colts. They looked at each other, then at Edge and their hard eyes acknowledged the fact that they could have been dead if the half-breed had wanted it that way.

'Will change the plan though,' Edge went on as the man on the left opened his mouth to speak. 'If you breathe too loud or don't do like I say. Move over against the wall.'

He side-stepped out of their path and gestured with his head the way he wanted them to go. The men glanced into each others' faces again and reached a second tacit agreement. Tracked by the menace of the Winchester, they put their backs to the rear wall of the cell block and inched along it. Their right hands were rock steady above the butts of their holstered guns. The hard eyes in their mean-looking faces remained fixed upon the slow-turning figure of the tall half-breed.

'What *do* you plan, mister?' one of the black-garbed men rasped softly as Edge nodded for them to halt and stepped closer to them.

'Win me some money at poker,' the half-breed answered evenly, taking care not to devote too much attention to the man on the left – the one whose head and shoulders were in front of the barred window of the kid's cell.

Hiram's face was hidden by the Devil's Disciple, but his hands and arms came into view, snaking out through the bars at either side of the man's head.

'I mean for us?' the man croaked, blinking.

'Hoping your future's clear cut,' Edge muttered.

Hiram had the razor clenched in his right hand. His left curled in and hooked over the collar of his victim's jacket. As he jerked his victim hard against the bars, the man vented a snarl.

His partner swung to stare at him.

Both went for their guns.

Edge moved in close.

Hiram's right hand went across in front of his man, then streaked back again. The snarl became a gasp, then a moist retch. Blood gushed from the gaping wound in the throat and sprayed from the wide mouth.

Edge turned his body sideways on to the second man and thrust the Winchester forward and upwards. The gunman's mouth was open, ready to scream – perhaps a warning or perhaps a cry of fear. Then the muzzle of the rifle stabbed between the gaping lips. His Colt was clear of the holster, but Edge brought up a knee and jerked it forward, to trap the wrist of the gun hand against the wall. Then he powered both hands in the same direction. The head of the Devil's Disciple crunched against the wall of the cell block. The back of his skull caved in, the rifle muzzle burst through the tissue on the inside of his throat, and his teeth were shattered by the metal of the rifle barrel as he clamped his mouth shut in death.

As Edge stepped back, withdrawing the Winchester amid a spray of blood, the man collapsed to the base of the wall.

Then the half-breed whirled, towards new sounds alien to the blizzard. His cold-pinched, leather-textured face was still set in the killer grimace, but abruptly his expression became neutral. For he recognised the bulky figure of the Baron emerging from the sleet, leading two black stallions by the reins. Both horses were saddled.

'Trouble?' the Englishman asked with just a hint of tension to mar his attempt at indifference to the danger that surrounded him.

'We handled it,' the kid growled.

'And you can leave go now, Hiram,' Edge told him, canting the rifle to his shoulder.

'Number three,' the youngster said, and released his hold on the coat collar of the man with the gaping throat wound. Then, as the body crumpled, he turned the razor so that the wooden handle was towards the half-breed. 'Like you been telling people, Edge. I learn real fast, don't I?'

Edge accepted the razor and stooped to wipe the blade on the jacket of one of the dead men. 'Yeah, Hiram. You're real sharp.'

'Beat a rug,' the kid exclaimed as the Baron approached the window and started to tie two lengths of rope to the bars. The other ends were lashed to the horns of the saddles cinched to the horses. 'Didn't figure you to get involved in something like this.'

The Englishman ignored him and looked at Edge. 'Two men were guarding the livery. They are merely work for the undertaker now.'

'How?' Edge asked.

'With my sword, sir. Tallis will attribute the crime to you. And with just two mounts missing, will assume the obvious.'

Edge nodded and moved to soothe the horses, which were restless in the wind and sleet. Then, as the Englishman finished tying the ropes, the tall, broad figure of Fyson emerged from the alley.

'All set, cousins?' he drawled.

As the Baron nodded, Edge crossed to the window and eyed the kid grimly through the bars.

'Room five, Hiram. And only use that gun if you have to.'

'I don't like it,' the kid muttered sullenly, gripping Edge's Colt which he had slid into one of his holsters. He looked beyond the half-breed, to where the Baron and Fyson had swung astride the two horses.

'It could be a lot of fun,' Edge answered. 'If you let Virginia know how rich you are.'

'Those two men dead?' Fyson asked as Edge used a free

stirrup to swing up on the horse behind the big ex-lawman.

'It bother you, feller?'

'I can't condone wanton killing, cousin.'

'A depleted enemy is a lesser enemy,' the Baron said.

'Cold-blooded murder makes you no better than they are,' Fyson insisted gruffly.

'I'm better than they are now, feller,' Edge muttered. 'Alive's got to beat dead. Let's go.'

He took a one-handed grip around Fyson's waist as the big man and the Baron backed their horses close to the rear wall of the cell block, putting as much slack as possible into the ropes.

'There will not be much time, son,' the Baron told Hiram.

'I won't be just standing here admiring the view, feller,' the kid answered.

'Now!' Fyson rasped.

He and the Baron thudded their heels into horseflesh, cracked reins, and yelled at the tops of their voices. The stolen stallions added to the explosion of sound with snorts of alarm – and lunged away from the wall.

They had taken only three strides into the gallop when the ropes stretched taut. They faltered at the abrupt force trying to halt them, but the window submitted to the combined strength of the two spooked horses. The bars were set into strips of iron at the top and bottom which in turn were embedded in cement. And it was the entire grille that wrenched free, springing out of the wall in a shower of cement fragments.

As the set of bars thudded to the ground and started to be dragged through the mud, Fyson and the Baron yanked on the hitch and the ropes uncurled from around the saddle horns and fell away.

Edge directed his gaze and the rifle back at the cell block, and saw Hiram Rydell scrambling through the enlarged hole where the bars had held him prisoner a moment before. At that moment, the cell block was lit by light spilling from the law office as the door was flung open. There was an angry yell and a shot, but Edge saw the kid land sure footed and move into a smooth sprint.

Then, just before the blizzard hurled its veiling curtain of driving sleet across the rear of the cell block, the half-breed exploded one shot for effect. And then there was nothing to see but the blackness of night streaked with needling arrows of dirty whiteness. If any more shots were fired, the crack of gunfire was masked by the lashing storm and the hoofbeats of the galloping stallions.

As they raced towards the chasm north of High Mountain, Fyson moved ahead of the Baron and changed course, signalling his intention with a long-armed wave. They rode west, still at the gallop, bodies leaning into the storm that obliterated all sign of their passage.

Riding virtually blind with only his knowledge of the local terrain to guide him, the towering ex-sheriff veered on to a new course that took them south, around the tent town and then up a wagon track between the fields – so there would be no tell-tale trail of trampled crops to show the way they had gone.

As the steepness of the slope became more severe, the horses were given slack rein to set their own pace. They were walking, steam from their lathered flanks merging with the vapour of their breath, as the rim of the basin was achieved.

Fyson signalled a halt and all three men dismounted.

'Your problem solved, cousin,' the tall man said to Edge as they moved around the rim towards the pass.

'One of them, feller,' Edge answered, blowing on his cold hands as he wedged the Winchester between his elbow and hip. 'Still a matter of the ten grand I'm out.'

'Ten grand?'

'Long story. But to have a chance at it, I figure my interests are mutual with yours.'

Fyson looked hard at the half-breed, then shrugged. And turned to the Baron who was striding along on the other side of him. 'What exactly is *your* interest in this business, cousin?'

'My son and his wife were small ranchers in Texas,' the Englishman replied, slowly, his tone grim. 'They banded together with some others to hire Tallis and his band of thugs – to escort a cattle drive north to Kansas. A thousand head of animals were rustled and my son had the misfortune to discover Tallis was responsible. Now my son is dead. Trampled by the stolen cattle.'

They were almost at the pass now, walking slowly and cautiously. Talking in low tones as they peered ahead, Fyson looking for landmarks while Edge and the Baron searched for signs of danger through the blizzard.

'I was not sure of the kind of man you were, sir,' the Englishman continued. 'Which was why I maintained my act as a drunken fool and coward until the very last.'

'I knew, cousin,' Fyson growled as they turned into the pass. 'Guessed it the moment he walked into my office with that crazy kid in the fancy clothes. Saw it for sure the way he handled those two on the street. Not the kind I'd choose, but there's no one else available.'

'In addition to me, sir,' the Baron pointed out.

'You're not proved yet, cousin.'

The Englishman's voice became as hard and cold as the steel of his sword. 'A man does not gain field promotion in the British army from sub-lieutenant to colonel on the North-West Frontier of India without proving himself, sir,' he pronounced.

'I didn't see it proved,' Fyson answered curtly.

They had gone through the pass and the ex-sheriff signalled a halt at the base of a tall escarpment where the cliff face was cleaved by a narrow split. The blizzard raged with increased intensity through the narrow, boulder-strewn pass. But the sounds coming through the gap in the escarpment were even louder and they had a shrill quality almost like human screams.

'Gully beyond here,' Fyson explained. 'Finishes at the far end in a cave. Called Livermore Hole. Named after an army captain who sheltered his troop in there way back. Twenty men out making a survey. Before High Mountain was built. Massacred by a war party of Utes. Story goes it's haunted and you can hear why that rumour started. Always makes those damn noises when a norther blows.'

'Sounds as full of wind as you are,' Edge muttered.

Fyson ignored the comment. 'Most local people won't come near this place, which is as good a reason as any for Tallis to pick it, I guess. Two hundred yards down the gully to the cave. We got them like rats in a trap if they're not expecting us, cousin. Can pick us off like apples in a barrel if they are.'

'Won't find out which by standing out here,' Edge pointed out.

'One point, cousins,' Fyson said quickly, and shifted his steady gaze from the face of Edge to the Baron and back again. 'Town will want me back as sheriff when they find out they been duped by Tallis. So I intend to act like I still had a badge on my chest.'

'In what way, sir?' the Baron asked.

'I've been the lawman here for twenty years and I've never killed a culprit in making an arrest. I'd like things to stay that way, cousins – if it is possible.'

All around them, the norther swirled and gusted, the sounds of its fury seeming to rise by the moment. And the eerie moans and whines that it created in the gully and cave sounded like cries of awesome warning.

'You can give your way a spin, High Fy,' Edge muttered as he moved towards the narrow gap in the cliff face. 'But I don't figure you've a ghost of a chance.'

Chapter Ten

THE men moved cautiously in a line of three along the gully, a Remington, a Winchester and a drawn sword ready to blast and thrust at the as yet unseen enemy.

Darkness and driving sleet reduced visibility to just a couple of yards and the noise of the blizzard masked the sound of footfalls to even their own ears. Then, in the blackness streaked with white ahead, they saw an orange glow – brightening with each step they took towards it. Closer still they caught the scent of woodsmoke from the fire, and the surrounding darkness looked even blacker in contrast with the flickering flames.

Abruptly, the three intruders experienced the almost euphoric luxury of being sheltered from the needling sleet, hearing voices against the moans of the wind.

'Call.'

'Raise ten.'

'Ten and up another ten.'

'I'm out.'

'Twenty to see what you got.'

'Full house. Aces and tens.'

'Beats three of a lousy kind.'

Edge was flanked by the Baron on his right and Fyson on his left. All three had halted just inside the threshold of the cave, taking time to allow their eyes to adjust to the darkness spread around the glowing fire. It took only a few moments, and then they were able to pick out shapes and movement.

Rollo Stone's white nightshirt-clad form was on the right of the fire. He was stretched out on his side, with his ankles bound and his hands tied behind his back. His eyes were blindfolded and his teeth gleamed in a grimace of pain or fear or a mixture of the two. Behind him was a heap of saddles and bedrolls and beyond this the four horses were hobbled. Grummond and the two other Devil's Disciples were sitting cross-legged on the other side of the fire. They had coffee mugs and piles of pebbles in front of them and the winner of the game raked pebbles from the centre to add to his pile. Another player gathered up the cards and started a new deal.

After the wet, neutral smell of the blizzard, the scents within the cave were strong. Horseflesh and horse droppings. Leather and woodsmoke. Coffee and unwashed bodies. Human excrement.

As their eyes became accustomed to the brightness and shadow after so long looking at just darkness, the trio of intruders inched into the area of fireglow that already encompassed the Devil's Disciples.

'Threes wild,' the dealer announced, grinning as he finished the deal and looking up.

He saw the newcomers and his grin became a fixed grimace of terror.

'A little mad, is all,' Edge growled.

'You're under arrest!' Fyson snarled.

The other two black-garbed men twisted from the waist and all three went for their guns.

'Goddamn it!' Fyson groaned, and squeezed the trigger of his Remington.

His bullet plunged into the heart of the man who had been facing the cave mouth. The man flipped out on to his back, gun spinning away as a spurt of crimson sprayed from the wound.

Edge fired the Winchester at the same time and hit his man in the temple. The bullet exited on the other side of his head amid a welter of crimson and the lighter coloured gore of brain tissue. As the corpse toppled, knees spasming up to the chest, the Baron leapt forward. His trailing leg moved into a

106

kick action and the boot lifted flaming kindling from the fire.

It was Grummond who felt the searing flames on his flesh as he struggled frantically to uncross his legs.

'Die, sir!' the Englishman bellowed, springing away from the fire to crash his feet to the ground in front of Grummond.

'One's real wild,' Edge muttered, pumping the Winchester's action, but curling his finger around the guard rather than the trigger.

Grummond's hair and the back of his jacket were smouldering. But he saw the more lethal threat of the enraged man standing before him and tracked his Colt to aim.

The sword swung and in a fraction of a second, Grummond's arm was slit open from shoulder to wrist. As his coat and shirt sleeves parted to show the terrible wound, the revolver fell from a hand greased by warm blood.

The injured man screamed.

'That's enough, goddamn it!' Fyson roared above the sound of agony and the moaning wind.

But the Baron, his bewhiskered face stony, as if carved from red-stained granite, was enclosed in a private world of vengeance that admitted nothing except his own desires and the object of those desires.

Grummond had fallen on to his back. The sand of the cave floor smothered the fire in his jacket, but his hair ignited with a burst of flame. His shrill scream rose to a girlish pitch.

'I said enough!' Fyson snarled as the Baron swung a leg to straddle the agonised Grummond.

This time the Englishman heard the demand. But his expression of unswerving determination did not alter as he lowered the point of the sword blade towards the contorted face of his victim.

'You must kill me to save this thug,' he answered.

Grummond's voice broke and he became silent as he stared at the descending blade. It was as if fear of the cold steel negated the agony of his mutilated arm and the searing pain of the flames licking at his scalp.

And the Devil's Disciple vented just a subdued sigh as the sword was thrust into his eye driving four inches of blade under the front of the skull and finding the brain. With the same grace he had shown in making the gentle thrust, the Baron withdrew the blade, twisting his wrist to lift Grummond's blood-filled eye from the dead socket – and to send it into the fire. It sizzled softly as it surrendered its moisture to the heat.

'I am finished now, sir,' the Englishman said, turning slowly to face the enraged glower and aimed Remington of the towering Fyson. 'For the moment, or for ever?'

His raised eyebrows added the query as he slid the blood-run blade into the stick.

The smell of scorched flesh blotted out all other smells in the cave, until Edge flipped off the lid of the coffee pot and lifted it from the fire to douse the contents over Grummond's burning hair.

Fyson remained rigid for a moment, then the tension drained from him, and he pushed the Remington back into the holster. His expression became a grimace of disgust as he looked down at the slaughtered corpse.

'He's better off dead, maybe.'

'Sir, have you ever seen a man crushed by stampeding cattle?' the Baron countered stiffly.

'Hey, what's going on?' Rollo Stone called, still terrified in the pitch darkness of his blindfold.

'The show, feller,' Edge answered as he crouched down beside the young musician and cut through the ropes and kerchief with his razor. 'If everyone keeps acting in concert.'

'Hey, they're Devil's Disciples!' Stone gasped, blinking against the firelight as he explored the bruise on his skull from the gun butt blow which had knocked him out in the hotel room. 'They snatched me?' He nodded in reply to his own question as his bright eyes supplied the evidence. Then his voice became a snarl. 'And I composed a new work dedicated to Tallis and his men!'

Edge had moved to the heap of gear to check on the supplies brought to the cave by the Devil's Disciples. For, after the tension had drained from him, his belly growled a protest that he had not eaten since noon.

During the explosion of violence, the wind had ceased to moan and whine through the cracks in the cave roof open to the weather, as if Nature had held its breath while it witnessed the carnage. But now the eerie noises began again – louder and more weird, sounding more than ever like the groans and wails of the disembodied spirits of the new and ancient dead.

'What on earth happened here?' Stone asked as he got shakily to his feet and stared in horror at the sprawl of corpses among the scattered playing cards and charred fire debris.

'High Fy just broke a record,' Edge answered evenly, coming erect and biting off a chunk of beef jerky.

'I don't expect consolation from you, cousin,' the former sheriff of High Mountain snarled.

Edge nodded to the man who had gone down in front of the exploding Remington. 'Ain't the one bleeding heart enough for you, feller?' he muttered.

'It was unavoidable, sir,' the Baron added calmly. 'And two things have been proved. My ability to do what must be done. And that sometimes the methods of the law to get what it wants differ from those of we two only in the matter of degree.'

He looked towards Edge for agreement and the half-breed nodded as he chewed on the dried meat.

'The brutal truth, feller,' he told the solemn-faced Fyson. 'Guess that makes the law's method the third degree.'

Chapter Eleven

EDGE looked down from the pass towards High Mountain and the chasm to the north of the single-street town. It was seventhirty on a bright, clear morning and despite the distance from the town and his altitude above it, he could see the component parts of the bustling scene in sharp detail.

The gusting cold of the norther and the icy assault of the sleet were distant memories of the black night becoming harder to recall with each moment that elapsed towards eight o'clock. For the blizzard had blown itself out in the early hours of the morning and the new day had dawned with a cloudless sky. Then, as soon as the sun showed its leading arc above the eastern ridges, it offered a promise of fierce heat to come. And already at such an early hour it was beginning to deliver on that promise.

But it was the tension of waiting as much as the warmth of the sun heat that squeezed the sweat beads from the half-breed's pores as he saw a Concord coach moving eastwards along the street below.

The town was as crowded this morning as it had been when he first looked down at it from the pass. But there was a difference now, outside of the fact that the scene was lit by the sun rather than oil lamps. For almost everyone except those aboard the coach were heading for the same ultimate destination, hurrying towards a pine-flanked pathway that led from the rear of the church down into the chasm.

In daylight, Edge could see that this chasm had steep, exposed rock walls on two sides, with the north and south sides formed by gentle, grass-covered slopes. The inevitable painted canvas signs hung from the rocky sides, too distant for the lean half-breed to read the lettering on them. But it was not hard to guess that they gave further information about the music festival which was to take place in the natural amphitheatre below the town. For a wooden stage had been built at the lowest point where the grassy slopes met and, neatly grouped on the platform, were a piano and a dozen or so chairs with music stands in front of them. To one side was a large tent decked out with coloured streamers.

Already, the lower stretches of the slopes were dotted with music lovers who had risen early to claim the best positions from which to watch the entertainment. And the audience was becoming thicker on the ground as the crowds were ushered into orderly rows by the familiar black-garbed Tallis men.

But not all the Devil's Disciples were on steward duty across the slopes. For, as the street became less crowded, Edge saw a group of a half dozen or so standing in front of the law office, watching the progress of the stage as it lumbered up the first gradient of the basin side.

Edge remained where he was for several more minutes. From the moment he first saw the Concord, he had recognised the unmistakable figure of Fyson riding in the guard's seat. Now, as the distance between the coach and the pass narrowed, he saw that the overweight, tobacco chewing Augie was in control of the four-horse team. There was no way he could look inside the Concord but, as he withdrew into the pass, he saw that the Devil's Disciples in the chasm had started up the slope towards the town.

Midway through the pass, the half-breed pumped the action of the Winchester and crouched behind a rock, his burnished features set in an expression of mild satisfaction. Because everything he had seen so far augured well for the battle plan which had been formed as he, Fyson, the Baron and Stone had crouched around the fire in the eerie, body-strewn cave.

It was not a plan he would have devised had he been working alone, and the Baron had also voiced reservations. But the

111

towering ex-sheriff had insisted upon reducing the risk of innocent blood being spilled.

Hoofbeats sounded on the trail through the pass and the big coach creaked on its springs.

'Reckon about here, cousin,' Fyson drawled.

'Whoooaaa, you ornery bastards!' Augie yelled at the team as Edge compressed his lips and cracked his eyes against the gritty dust raised by the slow-turning wheels.

He moved around from the rear to the side of the rock as the halting Concord rolled by. Then sucked in a deep breath and lunged forward, to sprint across fifteen feet of open space to reach the back of the coach.

'You see anythin' High Fy? a man called from inside, and swung open the door. The other door opened at the same time.

The Concord was rocking as the passengers moved to climb out, so that the additional motion as Edge hoisted himself on to the roof from the boot was not noticed.

'Nothing I wasn't expecting,' Fyson answered, turning fast on the seat and drawing his Remington. 'Just the two,' he told Edge, clashing eyes with the half-breed for an instant. Then he directed a glowering stare and the gun barrel at the black-garbed man halfway out of the Concord's right hand door.

'What in tarnation . . . !' Augie yelled, and a wad of tobacco shot from his wide lips.

'High Fy wants you alive, feller,' Edge said evenly to the man who had frozen with one foot on the step of the left side of the coach. 'Don't matter a damn to me, though.'

The half-breed had gone out at full stretch along the roof of the coach and drawn the razor from its pouch. As he spoke, he curved his hand around the front of the Devil's Disciple and pressed the blade of the razor against the leather-textured skin of the man's throat.

Both men had started to reach for their holstered Colts, but suddenly their arms seemed paralysed as one looked into a revolver muzzle at a range of six inches and the other felt finely honed steel touching his flesh.

'Friggin' hell, you again!' the overweight driver gasped and looked hurriedly around. 'Where's that crazy kid?'

Edge curled back his lips to show a wry grin. 'Told him we didn't need him to help us head 'em off at the pass.'

Augie shrugged, resigned to the unexpected happening when

the tall half-breed was nearby. 'Guess it ain't necessary for me to know what the hell's goin' on, uh?'

'He was set on driving,' Fyson put in. 'His company's coach and he's responsible for it.'

'Just figured on a little excitement,' Augie growled, climbing down and looking for the tobacco that had sprung from his mouth.

'Obliged if you'd get these fellers' guns,' Edge asked.

'Sure, sure,' Augie agreed. 'Like at the hold-up.'

'Where's Grummond and the others?' the man covered by Fyson croaked.

'Dead, cousin.'

'And it's catching around here,' Edge added blandly as the man below him stiffened.

Augie stood at arm's length to lift the Colt from the Devil's Disciple's holster. Then hurried around to the other side of the coach to claim the second man's weapon.

'Back inside,' Fyson ordered, and brandished the Remington.

'Same for you,' Edge instructed. 'You could get a sore throat out here in the morning air.'

Fyson sprang to the ground as Edge withdrew the threat of the razor and swung over the side of the coach. He replaced the razor in the pouch while he was in mid-air, and landed sure-footed with the Winchester aimed. But both prisoners were sitting rigid on the front-facing seat, fear showing through the sweat beads coursing their weathered features. There was a suitcase on the floor at their feet.

'That the money?' Edge asked.

Both men nodded.

'No problems?' The half-breed looked across the interior of the Concord to where Fyson was stooped outside the other open door.

'No, cousin. Storm held long enough for us to get into High Mountain without being seen. Stone reckons he can get that Box guy to go along with what we want. And that guy with the fancy foreign handle to his name is still as mean-minded as ever.'

'Tallis pretty full of himself – sending a couple of his boys.'

The two Devil's Disciples turned their heads this way and that, looking at Fyson and Edge in turn as each man contributed to the exchange. Augie had located the missing tobacco wad, dusted it off on his shirt front and was chewing on it again.

'Real confident, cousin. And more than happy to have me and the driver along as independent witnesses. Plans on giving Stone a guard of honour down to the stage.'

'Hiram?'

'Him and the whore still tucked up tight in bed when I last looked. Reckon he had a hectic night.'

'So he ain't just a tenderfoot any more?' the half-breed muttered sardonically as he climbed into the coach, slammed the door behind him and sat down on the seat opposite the two fearful gunmen. 'Used up enough time, I figure?'

Fyson nodded and used the Remington to close the door before he climbed up on the high seat. 'Turn her around and head back down, cousin,' he instructed Augie as the fat little driver reached his place and took up the reins. 'And be ready to jump off when we reach the town limits.'

'Not me, mister!' Augie retorted. 'I reckon you fellers are goin' up against the Tallis bunch, along with the Baron, that right?'

'You're outta your mind!' the blue-eyed Devil's Disciple growled as the team was urged into making a tight turn.

'You could be right, feller,' Edge muttered, tracking the Winchester from one man to the other and back again.

'Don't provoke him, Roy,' the black-garbed man with a scar on his jaw croaked.

'Didn't plan on this much excitement, I gotta admit that,' Augie yelled above the noise of the Concord and team. 'But I'll sure enjoy takin' a crack at Tallis and his bunch.'

'We are not doing it for fun, cousin,' the ex-sheriff told him.

Augie grinned, squeezing tobacco juice through his dark stained teeth. 'Last time I had a couple of guns stuck in my belt, they weren't there for fun. But I sure had me a whale of a time fightin' for the republic against old Santa Anna.'

'Remember the Alamo?' Edge asked the two prisoners conversationally as the Concord tilted on to the downgrade.

'You were a lot younger in those days, cousin!' Fyson pointed out above the increased noise of speed.

'Meant I had a lot more to lose,' Augie answered philosophically. 'What you want me to do, High Fy?'

As the ex-lawman explained the plan to Augie, Edge maintained his almost constant watch on the sweating Devil's

114

Disciples, sparing just the occasional fleeting glance for the town each time the Concord took a turn to bring High Mountain into view.

The single street was now empty of everyone except the group of black-garbed men in front of the law office. The doors of all the building along each side were firmly closed and the windows – glinting in reflection of the morning sunlight – looked like empty eyes, with no suggestion that there were human watchers behind them.

Beyond the town, the grassy slopes spreading down to the platform with its adjacent tent were thickly packed with the local citizens and the rich out-of-towners. The entire audience was watching the progress of the approaching Concord in silence. But there was an almost tangible quality of mounting excitement in the warm stillness. And a ripple of subdued noise broke, and then was immediately quelled, as the tuxedo-clad Duke Box moved out of the tent and on to the stage. He was carrying a bullhorn.

Edge saw all this from behind a casual attitude that was just a surface veneer. Underneath this, his muscles were tensed for fast action and his mind worked coolly on what those actions would have to be if he were going to survive the violence that would shortly explode on the peaceful scene.

'Smile, fellers,' he instructed his prisoners as the Concord rolled across the town limits.

The men grimaced with mixed fear and rage.

'You look like death,' Edge criticised, taking first pressure around the rifle trigger. 'And if that's how you feel, be happy to oblige.'

Both men showed their teeth with upturns of the mouthline at each corner and the half-breed realised it was as much as he could expect under the circumstances. And it was good enough, for the sun was shafting down from behind the coach and its interior was in shade.

'Ladies and gentlemen!' the voice of Duke Box bellowed as the Concord rolled within twenty yards of the law office. 'Mr Rollo Stone has been rescued from the evil men who kidnapped him. And here he comes. To open the High Mountain Festival of Fine Music. Playing, with his world famous quartet, a piece especially composed for this occasion – *Concerto for the Devil and his Disciples.*'

The grin of triumph on the ugly face of Ben Tallis

broadened, displaying his very white teeth and emphasising the cruel knife scars.

'How about that, Sol?' he rasped to his first lieutenant who stood beside him at the front of the group of black-garbed gunmen. Then, as Augie hauled on the reins without applying the brake, Tallis raised his voice: 'No problems, High Fy?'

'Not for me, cousin,' Fyson growled. Then, under his breath: 'I hope.'

'Up and out,' Edge snapped. 'Ain't against shooting fellers in the back.'

Diagonally across the street from the law office, the double doors of the De Cruz Livery Stable were flung wide and the flames of a burning torch flared in the shaded interior.

Up on the Concord seat, Fyson drew his Remington, the bulk of Augie's frame hiding the move from Tallis and his men.

Augie caught the signal and took a tighter grip on the reins.

Roy and his partner got hurriedly to their feet, the man with the scar swinging open the door of the coach.

Uproar exploded suddenly from the open air concert hall. At first, as the tall, slender Rollo Stone led his group of musicians from the tent to the platform, there were gasps and shrieks of surprise and shock. Then a burst of delighted applause. Finally, a tumult of cheering that was abruptly curtailed – to allow the pure music of four violins to penetrate melodiously through the warm air of a morning that was suddenly heavy with the menace of violence about to break.

'What the – !' Tallis snarled, his smile and those on the faces of his men becoming enraged scowls.

'Ben! Sokalski snarled. 'Somebody messin' with our horses again!'

In the livery, Baron Finn-Jenkins brandished the flaming torch at the handsome black stallions he had freed from their stalls. And, snorting in terror, the animals lunged at a gallop for the open street.

'Ain't nobody gonna mess with Disciples' horses and get away with it!' a man roared.

'Don't just stand there,' Edge rasped. 'They're playing your tune.'

Bracing himself against the back of the seat, he raised both feet from the floor and bent his knees. Then he sprang, his

116

legs straight, and the heels of his boots slammed into Roy's back.

'We been friggin' had!' Tallis yelled, going for his gun.

The men behind him went for the draw.

The two black-garbed men aboard the Concord were sent crashing out of the open doorway as Augie cracked the reins and the team lunged into movement.

Edge fired the first shot as he dropped down on to one knee and aimed across the falling forms of the screaming men he had pushed out.

Fyson was just a split-second later in squeezing the trigger of the Remington, the crack of his gun lost amid the fusillade exploded by the grouped Devil's Disciples.

Two men died as the Rollo Stone Quartet played the opening *lento* movement of the *Concerto for the Disciples of the Devil*.

For Roy and the other luckless man who had been sent to the pass were caught in the hail of lead instinctively directed towards the coach as it moved forward from a standstill.

Two more staggered under the impact of crippling wounds as the shots of Edge and Fyson – fired for effect with no chance to take aim from the jolting Concord – spun into flesh amid the panicked and enraged group of Devil's Disciples.

Augie lost his tobacco chew again as bullets cracked about him and he wrenched on the reins to send the team into a tight turn. Behind the snorting horses, the coach swayed dangerously to the side – canting up on to two wheels as it tore into the alley between the law office and the church.

Sprawled low across the roof, Fyson fanned the Remington hammer to send a spray of bullets towards the enemy.

The black-garbed men who had lunged away from the law-office façade were driven back by flying lead and the pumping hooves of horses spooked out of the livery.

Edge was slid along the seat by the tilt of the crazy turn. As he slammed against the padded side, he reached out a hand and turned the handle of the door. The door flapped wide and he powered out through the opening as the Concord bounced back on all four wheels again.

Augie slammed on the brake and acrid smoke streamed from between the wood blocks and metal rims. Dust billowed from under the sliding wheels and flailing hooves.

Edge hit the ground with his feet, but could not brace himself against the forward momentum of his exit from the Concord. He ran for three strides, then pitched through the dust cloud. Bullets dug divots from the ground around him and snagged at his clothing.

Every part of his lean form suffered jarring pain as he slammed into the ground, and the wind whooshed up from his lungs to whistle through his clenched teeth.

But his desire to survive sublimated pain, and strength was forced into his punished muscles. Strength to power him into a roll, over and over until he came up hard against the wooden front of the church.

Splinters showered down on him as bullets cracked across the alley mouth to rip into the clapboard.

His eyes were out of focus from the spin of the roll and tears squeezed from his eyes from the gritty dust. But his hearing was still unimpaired. He heard the violin quartet as the pace of the music built from *lento* to *allegro*. The melody was counterpointed by the crash of gunfire and the thud of bullets into the woodwork close to him. And voices.

'The bastards!' From Sokalski.

'Kid!' A woman's voice – the whore, Virginia – shrieked from the open window of the saloon's second storey.

'Get the back, cousin!' Fyson.

'You varmints! I'll cover you partner! I'll fill these no-good critters full of hot lead.'

Edge shook his head and his vision cleared. His back was against the angle of the church front and the ground, feet under the steps of the sidewalk where it restarted after breaking for the alley. The dust raised by the panicked horses was settling as the animals galloped off the street and out on to the trail.

He saw the heads and naked torsos of Hiram and the whore at the open window of the hotel. The young dude was using the half-breed's Colt to send fast shots towards the front of the law office. There was an excited grin on his face, contrasting starkly with the anguish expressed by the naked woman at his side.

Then he saw the bewhiskered Baron, on one knee in the doorway of the meeting hall – firing a Winchester with the same brand of controlled rage that he had handled the sword in the cave up at the pass.

The barrage from the kid and the Englishman had driven the Devil's Disciples into cover and the two kept up the fusillade as Edge pushed himself on to all fours and then scuttled forward across the mouth of the alley.

More shots sounded at the rear of the law office and cell block and the half-breed glanced down the alley as he dived under the sidewalk in front of the building.

The Concord had not slithered to a halt until it was on the back lots of the flanking buildings and Fyson and Augie were now using it as cover from which to explode shots at the hole in the cell-block wall caused by Hiram's gaol-break.

Abruptly the shooting ended as Edge lay in the shade of the sidewalk planking and sucked in deep breaths of warm, dusty air. But, as the ice-blue slits of his eyes raked the street, the violin music of *Concerto for the Disciples of the Devil* was not the only sound in the deep basin. For, during this brief lull in the gunfight, the fast-moving melody competed with the shrieks, screams and yells of the terrified audience.

'Stay back!' Fyson bellowed, his voice all but drowned by the exclamations from a multitude of throats.

The kid ducked back out of sight, dragging the whore with him. The Baron fed fresh shells through the loading gate of the Winchester. Edge blinked sweat beads from his eyelids and looked impassively at the two horse carcasses and four black-garbed bodies sprawled on the grey dust under the yellow sunlight.

He looked at the blood-smeared bodies of the men with the same lack of emotion as he had viewed the ravaged remains of the cougar under the mesa, his hooded eyes as cold as they had been when they raked over the other corpses that marked his trail from that mesa to this street.

'Watch out!' Virginia shrieked.

Hiram had reloaded the Colt with shells taken from Edge's saddlebags. And he had put on his ten gallon hat. It looked more incongruous than ever atop his youthful face as he appeared at the window again.

'Here's your one way tickets to Boot Hill, you lousy – '

He got off a single shot that shattered the glass panel of the law office door.

Then a fusillade of answering fire exploded from the already smashed window of the building.

Hiram's chest, pale and hairless, was abruptly marked by half a dozen dark holes. He died without a scream, the impact of the bullets knocking him backwards. He crashed into the

119

naked whore and bounced forward, blood spurting from the wounds to slide slickly down his flesh.

Virginia shrieked a profanity. Hiram's crumpling body hit the window sill and he folded forward over it. His hat fell off as the Colt dropped from his lifeless hand. He tipped out through the window, slammed against the saloon canopy, and thudded to the street, naked except for his fancy boots, their rhinestone trimmings sparkling in the sunlight.

Just a flicker of emotion showed in the ice-blue slits of the half-breed's hooded eyes now. But the moment of pain that showed was physical – caused by the movement of a bruised shoulder rather than the mental anguish of watching the reckles young dude die. And it was followed by a fleeting smile that brought to the surface all the latent cruelty that lurked within the lean body of the man.

'You've gone as far west as you can go, Hiram,' he muttered against a snarling cheer from inside the law office.

Edge's sardonic humour was not triggered by the violent death of the naïve youngster from New York's West Side. Rather, it as his response to the killing; which was totally negative.

There had been an affinity with, and a liking for, Hiram Rydell: but neither were strong enough to penetrate the half-breed's defensive barrier against the kind of involvement that could lead to more than a shallow relationship. Thus, Edge could concentrate entirely on the reason he had come to this single street town in the Sangre de Cristo Mountains.

Plain and simple money, which a man could gain and lose with equanimity for there was always more to replace that which was lost.

People could not be replaced. Not Jamie, not Beth and certainly not his own lost youth as epitomised in the unlikely form of Hiram Rydell. But if a man wanted to attain something that was vitally important to him, his mind had to be free of the influence of side-issues, and a human relationship of any depth could be a deadly side-issue.

Edge wanted ten thousand dollars, an amount which had taken on a special significance in his life. There had been that much hidden in a small Mexican town called Montijo – sufficient for Edge to make a new start and help insulate him from the tragedy of Jamie's death. But rats reached the money before the half-breed. Then there had been the second ten thousand, paid to him by a woman who had revived memories of Beth. The woman could not be his, and the money had been put further out of reach than its donor.

Between these two opportunities to paste over an emotional void with the richness of money was a chain of time with the links forged of savage violence and harsh suffering. A time during which so much else had been won and lost with no ultimate gain except continued survival – and survival with no aim until the mind of the half-breed fixed upon this goal.

The audience in the open-air concert arena had quietened, but through the now up-tempo strains of the *Concerto for the Disciples of the Devil* came another sound: the voices of the crowd were silent, but their running feet on the grassy slopes seemed to vibrate the ground of the entire basin.

'Get back you crazy fools!' Fyson yelled.

Edge experienced a stirring of foreboding in his coldly working mind.

'Bust outta the back!' he heard Tallis snarl. 'Get in the crowd!'

Footfalls thudded on the floorboards.

'Jesus Christ!' Augie screamed.

Revolver shots exploded – towards the hole in the cell block and from it.

'We need some help, cousins!' Fyson shrieked, fear withdrawing every hint of the drawl from his voice.

Edge started to roll out from under the sidewalk, his actions triggered entirely by self-interest, brain unclouded by any desire to revenge the death of Hiram Rydell.

Baron Finn-Jenkins broke from the doorway of the meeting hall, firing and pumping the action of the Winchester.

'You killed my son!' he roared, his inflamed passion for vengeance keeping him on a straight course to his objective.

Edge halted his roll – sprawled on his back and looking up between gaps in the sidewalk planking.

Two men had not rushed to the rear of the building. They stepped across the threshold of the front doorway now, fanning their Colts.

Had he zig-zagged and bobbed, the paunch Englishman might have evaded the bullets. And his mistake cost him his life. He was hit three times in the face, pulled up short, stood for a moment, and corkscrewed to the ground. Blood from his pulped nose and the two holes in his forehead rained down on his fallen

121

Winchester – adding fresh stains to those Luke had made on the stock.

There was not enough clearance under the sidewalk for Edge to bring his rifle to the aim.

'Where's that bastard – ' Sokalski snarled.

Edge powered out from cover, again halting the roll with his back pressed to the ground. He aimed from the shoulder, fired, worked the action and fired again.

'Sometimes get under folks' feet,' he muttered as Sokalski and Nye plunged through the doorway, trailing twin arcs of blood from their punctured jaws.

The bullets burst clear at the tops of their skulls and gore sprayed along the door lintel. Drops of it splashed on Edge as he scrambled erect and leapt across the sidewalk and into the office.

Sokalski and Nye brought the total of dead inside to three. Unfeeling flesh was soft beneath Edge's feet as he advanced across the office to the open doorway into the cell block. Glass from the shattered windows crunched. Gunfire masked the sound.

Gunsmoke stung his eyes and assaulted his nostrils.

There were two more inert Devil's Disciples in the cell block. Tallis and four more were standing at each side of the enlarged aperture where the barred window had once been.

Between their heads and shoulders, Edge could see a part of the Concord – the front half, with its woodwork holed and splintered by bullets. Augie and Fyson continued to blast shots from the cover of the coach, which rocked as the surviving horse of the team struggled to get up off its side, dragged down by the dead weight of three carcases.

Bullets spat against the outside wall and cracked through the opening to ricochet off cell bars.

The black-garbed men took a signal from the ugly Tallis and sent a volley of gunshots towards the Concord.

Fyson was standing on the spokes of a front wheel, clinging to the cover of the seat. He leaned into the open for another shot, and his craggy face exploded crimson spray and chunks of blood-moist flesh as he was hit by every bullet in the fusillade.

The *Concerto for the Disciples of the Devil* moved into the crescendo of its finale as the massively built former sheriff was flung from the coach and crashed limply to the ground.

'They got High Fy!' Augie shrieked from inside the Concord. 'Oh, my God!'

'Just for the record, you fellers want to surrender?' Edge asked as the men at the far end of the cell block prepared to burst out from the hole into the open.

They whirled and the half-breed read their intent in the enraged eyes. He fired twice while still erect and two men died, their falling corpses banging against the other men and spoiling the aim of smoking guns.

His hand pumping the action as fast as hot metal would allow, he fired again from a crouch. A bullet grazed his earlobe as a third black-garbed man crumpled.

'We had it friggin' made!' Ben Tallis snarled, drawing a bead on the half-breed as Edge threw himself into a sprawl.

Edge was committed to a shot at the second survivor. His bullet found the man's heart and Tallis squeezed the Colt trigger.

Just as he had experienced the foreboding while lying under the sidewalk, now the half-breed sensed his ruling fate would cause the firing pin of the revolver to fall against a spent shellcase.

The gun clicked.

Another one fired.

His knife-punished face contorted by depthless fury, Tallis lunged forward, hurling the empty Colt away from him. Drops of blood hit the body-littered floor behind him.

'I got him!' Augie yelled in delight as Tallis powered out of the cell.

Edge pushed himself up. With an animalistic snarl, Tallis increased his speed, long arms reaching out and hands clawed.

The Winchester was only half-pumped when the hands closed over the barrel.

The half-breed made his choice. While his left hand maintained a tight grip around the frame of the rifle, his right streaked to the nape of his neck.

Tallis came to an abrupt halt and wrenched on the rifle barrel. Edge fought the challenge for a split second, then released his hold.

The roar from Tallis's throat now had a note of triumph as he swung the Winchester back, then started it forward. Edge bobbed down, leaned forward, and drove his right hand upwards.

The *Concerto for the Disciples of the Devil* came to an abrupt end and, for the first time since they had performed in public, the Rollo Stone Quartet received no applause.

Edge ducked his head under the vicious swing of the rifle. And his hand streaked up between the extended arms of Tallis – to drive the whole length of the razor's blade into the centre of the man's throat.

The eyes of the doomed man bulged to the extent where they seemed on the point of popping from their sockets. Then there was a wet sound in his throat.

Edge stepped back, withdrawing the blade and plucking his Winchester from Tallis's weakened grasp with his free hand.

The man tottered for a moment, then died and crumpled to the floor, showing the blood-ringed hole among the studs which spelled out his name on the back of his jacket.

'I didn't finish him, uh?' Augie called hoarsely as he appeared in the jagged hole, and pushed a fresh chew of tobacco into his mouth.

'He was dead, I guess,' Edge allowed. 'I just made him lie down.'

Then he turned and walked across the wrecked, acrid-smelling law office and out on to the street.

'It figured we was gonna lose some, Mr Edge,' the stage driver said as he followed the ambling half-breed.

'Nothing is for nothing, feller,' Edge answered evenly as he reached the far side of the street and stooped to pick up his Colt and slide it into his holster.

'I tried to stop him,' Virginia called down from the window. Her nakedness was now draped by a blanket but the expression of shock remained frozen on her face. 'He didn't have the time to do more than put on his boots and grab the gun when the shootin' started. I tried to stop him.'

There were tears welling in her eyes and she spoke with a catch in her voice.

'No charge, ma'am,' Edge told her as he shifted his hooded eyes from the whore to the corpse of Hiram Rydell. Above his bullet-ravaged chest the youngster's face was fixed in a grimace of excitement that looked strangely fake on his youthful, blond-fuzzed features.

'He was a crazy kid,' the whore croaked. 'But I liked him one hell of a lot. It's a lousy crime he had to die this way.'

The first people from the open air concert had appeared on

the street and the crowd was growing larger by the moment. Edge glanced around at them and, from the looks on their wan faces – of horror and deep shock – he knew the earlier feeling of foreboding had been valid. For there was now too much death in this small town – out back of the law office and cell block, inside the building and on the street. A final score of violence to a troubled time that added up to more carnage than these rich people from sheltered city backgrounds would be able to take. Or perhaps it was just that there was no longer any protection for that portion of their wealth they had brought with them. Whichever, the High Mountain Festival of Fine Music – together with all its side trappings – had begun and ended this blood-soaked morning.

'Sure is,' Augie said, dribbling tobacco juice as he controlled the nervous tic in his right cheek. 'But I guess the kid died where he would have wanted – out here in the West that was sure wild today.'

'Better than that,' Edge replied, then worked saliva into his mouth and spat it out with the after-taste of killing.

'Better?' the whore exclaimed tearfully. 'There's nothin' good about a nice young kid like him gettin' killed.'

Edge took a final, bleak-eyed glance at Hiram Rydell, nude except for his rhinestone-studded footwear. 'Died the way he would have wanted – with his boots on.'

THE END

THE GEORGE G. GILMAN · APPRECIATION SOCIETY ·

---◆---

The George G. Gilman Appreciation Society

---◆---

is intending to begin in
November/December 1976,
and is taking on members now.
For full details, please send a SAE to
Mr. David Whitehead, 4, Key Close,
Tower Hamlets, London, E.1. 4HG.

---◆---

NEL BESTSELLERS

War

T027 066	COLDITZ: THE GERMAN STORY	*Reinhold Eggers*	50p
T020 827	COLDITZ RECAPTURED	*Reinhold Eggers*	50p
T020 584	THE GOOD SHEPHERD	*C. S. Forester*	40p
T012 999	PQ 17 – CONVOY TO HELL	*Lund & Ludlam*	30p
T026 299	TRAWLERS GO TO WAR	*Lund & Ludlam*	50p
T025 438	LILLIPUT FLEET	*A. Cecil Hampshire*	50p
T018 032	ARK ROYAL	*Kenneth Poolman*	40p
T027 198	THE GREEN BERET	*Hilary St George Saunders*	50p
T027 171	THE RED BERET	*Hilary St George Saunders*	50p

Western

T017 893	EDGE 12: THE BIGGEST BOUNTY	*George Gilman*	30p
T023 931	EDGE 13: A TOWN CALLED HATE	*George Gilman*	35p
T020 002	EDGE 14: THE BIG GOLD	*George Gilman*	30p
T020 754	EDGE 15: BLOOD RUN	*George Gilman*	35p
T022 706	EDGE 16: THE FINAL SHOT	*George Gilman*	35p
T024 881	EDGE 17: VENGEANCE VALLEY	*George Gilman*	40p
T026 604	EDGE 18: TEN TOMBSTONES TO TEXAS	*George Gilman*	40p
T028 135	EDGE 19: ASHES AND DUST	*George Gilman*	40p
T029 042	EDGE 20: SULLIVAN'S LAW	*George Gilman*	45p

General

T017 400	CHOPPER	*Peter Cave*	30p
T022 838	MAMA	*Peter Cave*	35p
T021 009	SEX MANNERS FOR MEN	*Robert Chartham*	35p
T023 206	THE BOOK OF LOVE	*Dr David Delvin*	90p
T028 623	CAREFREE LOVE	*Dr David Delvin*	60p

Mad

S006 739	MADVERTISING	70p
N766 275	MORE SNAPPY ANSWERS TO STUPID QUESTIONS	70p
N769 452	VOODOO MAD	70p
S006 741	MAD POWER	70p
S006 291	HOPPING MAD	70p
